A COUNTRY BOY

MORE OSSIE STORIES

Earl McKenzie

LMH PUBLISHING LIMITED

All LMH Publishing Limited titles are available at special quantity discounts for bulk purchases for sales promotion, premiums, fund-raising, educational or institutional use.

Editor: K. Sean Harris
Cover Artwork: Earl McKenzie
Cover Design: Roshane Mullings
Book Design, Layout & Typesetting: Roshane Mullings

Published by LMH Publishing Limited
Suite 10-11, Sagicor Industrial Park
7 Norman Road
Kingston C.S.O., Jamaica
Tel.: 876-938-0005; 876-938-0712
Fax: 876-759-8752
Email: lmhbookpublishing@cwjamaica.com
Website: www.lmhpublishing.com

Printed in the U.S.A.   ISBN: 978-976-8245-83-0

NATIONAL LIBRARY OF JAMAICA CATALOGUING-IN-PUBLICATION DATA

Names: Mckenzie, Earl, author.
Title: A country boy: more Ossie stories / Earl Mckenzie.
Description: Kingston : LMH Publishing Limited, 2019.
Identifiers: ISBN 9789768245830.
Subjects: LCSH: Fiction. | Young adult fiction, Jamaican.
Classification: DDC 813 -- dc23.

CONTENTS

Dedication

For Trudy

THE HAIRCUT

"Ossie you need a trim," his mother said while washing dishes at the outside dresser, her back to him. "Look how your hair grow long so quick. You turning a Rasta or what?"

Ossie was at the dining table having breakfast. Mr. Llewellyn, his teacher, had told the class that boys needed twice as much food as girls do, and he was making use of the education he was receiving by digging into the roast yam and saltfish, and taking enthusiastic sips of the bissy tea.

"Uncle Phil will give you a trim," his mother continued.

"Uncle Phil!" exclaimed Ossie, speaking to his mother through the open door. "But he is not a barber!"

"He went to America as a farm worker and brought back some barbering tools. He wants to learn the trade."

"But why should he practise on me?" demanded Ossie.

"If he doesn't practise how can he learn? And better he practise on his nephew than on strangers."

This bit of information ruined Ossie's breakfast. Suddenly the yellow yam seemed cold and hard and the bissy had lost its flavour. What was he going to do? For the remaining days of the week Ossie did his chores and school work with the fear of that dreaded trim like a dark cloud above his head.

Ossie had nothing against Uncle Phil. He was a soft-spoken man who lived with his wife and four children on the sunset-side of the district. His stint as a farm worker in the U.S.A. had been his first opportunity to travel overseas and earn some foreign currency, and Ossie thought it was laudable that he wanted to learn another trade to supplement his income from farming. Whenever Ossie's mother wanted to prod his father, she would praise his brother Uncle Phil as a model of an enterprising man.

But Ossie would much prefer to get his hair cut at Prendy's as usual. Prendy was a dashing young man who owned a bicycle with two bells, two horns and even a speedometer. On Sunday mornings he cut hair under an ackee tree in his yard. He had a wooden sign on the tree which read: FRANK PRENDERGAST: TONSORIAL ARTIST. Prendy had a scrapbook with photographs which he cut from mostly American magazines, and his customers could choose the ones they wanted.

"I like cutting Ossie's hair," he once said to the waiting men and boys while he trimmed Ossie. "His haircut will sit down on his head for weeks before it starts to grow out of shape."

It was a pleasant chore going to Prendy's. He could listen to men and boys talk about the things that interested them: sports, politics, automobiles and women. Prendy's customers came from the neighbouring villages, and they began assembling from early in the morning ahead of the intensifying heat of the sun.

On the dreaded Sunday morning of the trim, Uncle Phil arrived before sunrise. He was a short and stocky man with brown skin and curly hair, and he was wearing his trademark khaki shirt and pants. He gripped the handle of the small black case with his barbering tools. The little case was so neat and mathematically precise it had 'foreign' written all over it. Ossie took a chair from the dining room and placed it under the small mango tree beside his mother's garden. Uncle Phil asked Miss Ona, Ossie's mother, for one of his father's old shirts to be used as an apron. Ossie sat down, and Uncle Phil draped him in the old white shirt. The massacre was about to begin.

Ossie felt the cold shear on the back of his neck. Then he could feel its coldness on his scalp as it moved upwards, removing his hair. Before long the sensation was on top of his head, and he could see tufts of his hair falling on the old shirt. Uncle Phil put away the shear and took out a pair of scissors. Ossie could hear the snipping. Then he could feel Uncle Phil lathering the back and sides of his head. Ossie could feel the clumsiness in Uncle Phil's hands as he began shaving with the very sharp razor.

"There you go," said Uncle Phil as he began removing the shirt-apron.

Ossie went into his parents' bedroom to look at himself in the mirror on the wall. He was devastated by what he saw. His hair had been reduced to some ugly blotches on his skull. Prendy's neat outline of his hair was no more. Gone was the handsome fellow that one of his aunts was fond of telling him that he was.

He went to the table for breakfast.

"That one should last a long time," said his mother as she served him fried dumplings and a cup of hot chocolate.

Maas Johnny, Ossie's father, looked at the haircut and said nothing, but Ossie thought he saw a slight twinkle in his eyes. Although Ossie loved fried dumplings made of flour and cornmeal, and eggs fried over and well done, he had difficulty enjoying his meal. The unsatisfactory haircut had given him a sense of loss.

"At least Uncle Phil charged less than Prendy," his mother said when she came to clear the dishes.

"Charge!" Ossie said to himself. "He gets paid for doing this to me!"

Later in the morning Ossie got dressed to go to Sunday school. His mother had put out his clothes on his bed. He put on his navy-blue pants, white shirt and necktie, and the pair of black shoes he had polished until they shone. Then he set off with his bible and hymnbook in his hand.

On the road he caught up with Paulette, the pretty daughter of the man everybody called Drunk Already. She had her hair in a pony-tail under a small white hat, and she wore a white dress. She too was carrying a bible and a hymnbook.

"I see you got a haircut, Ossie," she said. "Did it hurt?"

"Hurt! Of course not," replied Ossie. "Haircuts don't hurt."

He passed her walking quickly, and she had to increase her speed to keep up with him.

When they got to the churchyard Ossie felt very self-conscious, for it seemed as if everyone was noticing his haircut. He could see their gaze move from his clothes up to his face and hair. He went inside and sat in the children's section where Mrs. Roberts, a brown woman with rimless spectacles, was getting ready to teach the day's lesson.

"Cane row!" said a boy who was sitting behind him. "Ossie get cane row!"

He could hear the other boys chuckling. But Ossie did not turn to look. He stared straight ahead as he waited for the lesson to begin.

It was at school the following day that the real action started. Phonso, who sat beside Ossie in class, burst out laughing as soon as Ossie took his seat. "Ossie get into an accident with a barber!" he declared loud enough for the entire class to hear. The pupils in front turned to look at Ossie. "Accident!" continued Phonso, "and Ossie has no insurance!" There was laughter in the class. Ossie pointed his fist at Phonso's chin.

"Cut it out you two!" shouted Mr. Llewellyn from his desk. "Alphonso Dacres and Oswald Johnson, don't let me have to bring both of you up here! You are skating on thin ice!"

The laughter died down but an occasional chuckle could still be heard. With the roll call over Mr. Llewellyn began a round of mental arithmetic. The class began focusing on giving the quick answers to the problems he gave orally. Ossie's haircut was temporarily forgotten.

But during the recess the bigger boys descended on Ossie. They circled him and took turns smashing the back of his head with their open palms. "Smash!" they shouted after each successful landing of a stroke. But Ossie fought back with everything he had. He even managed to score a couple smashes of his own. When it became clear to the boys that he would resist their taunts and bullying, they eased up and soon left him alone.

As his hair grew the taunts ceased. He became absorbed in his school work and chores. But the spectre of Uncle Phil's haircuts continued to haunt him. Was he doomed to be the butt of taunts and violence each time he had a haircut?

"You need a haircut too," his mother said to his father one morning at breakfast. "Uncle Phil will fix you up."

"Over my dead body!" replied his father. "After what he did to Ossie, I wouldn't walk on the same side of the road with that man!"

"How can you say that about your own brother?" his mother said.

"Philip can borrow my jacket and my saw anytime. But he is not putting his hand in my hair."

"Then how is he going to learn? Didn't you have to learn carpentry? Did you build your first house just so?"

"Philip can practice anywhere he thinks. But not on my head."

"Perhaps he could practice on a mannequin," suggested Ossie.

"A what?" said his mother.

"You know those models they put clothes on in store windows?" continued Ossie. "I think that is what they call them. I could make some heads for him from coconuts."

"Yes, make Ossie teach him," said his father. "I would trust him with coconuts."

"I don't think Uncle Phil would be interested in that," said his mother. "You should consider his feelings."

"All the men he gave haircuts to are up in arms against him," said Maas Johnny. "All except Old Joe, and he is almost completely bald."

Ossie liked this turn of events, for he could now use his father's example in his arguments against his mother. He began saving his pocket money so he could pay for his next haircut at Prendy's, with his own money. His mother was more likely to relent if the haircut would be at no cost to her. His father's earning from carpentry was spasmodic, and his mother did not earn a great deal from her sewing and the vegetables she sold to higglers. He earned a little extra money from collecting and selling rat-cut cocoa to Maas Thom, the Chinese shopkeeper; sometimes he sold fruits to the higglers, and sometimes his relatives gave him money. His hair was growing steadily, and his anxiety was increasing. He saw the money he was saving as his only hope.

One day Uncle Phil came to visit, and Ossie overheard him discussing his plans with Miss Ona in the kitchen. He told her he didn't believe in putting all his eggs in one basket, and that one should try every little thing. That was why he had also brought back some shoemaking tools from the States, and that this would be his next endeavour. His mother told Uncle Phil he would have her full support. "As a matter of fact, one of Ossie's shoes needs fixing," she said.

His mother offered no resistance, and Ossie was light-footed on the Sunday morning he returned to Prendy's. It seemed like ages since he had last sat with the men and boys and listened to their stories. Prendy must have heard about Uncle Phil, for when Ossie sat in the barber's chair he said:

"I would have given the man some barbering lessons for free. Bread not sweet inna one man's mouth. But welcome back, Ossie. I going to give you one of the new styles today. Going to fix you up good, boy."

MAAS PENG

When Ossie arrived at Miss Lyn's shop one evening, the men who were playing dominoes on a table in the corner were having a good laugh.

"You mean it really happen?" asked Maas Kenny, a round-faced brown man, as he slapped a card hard on the table.

"Yes man," reflected Papa. He was wearing a tattered felt hat, had a pug-nose and chocolate skin. "It was during the two-week rain. Peng's wife, Miss Mirrie, kept telling him that there was no more shop-food in the house. Shop-food done. So he should go bush to look some food: a piece of yam, banana, breadfruit, anything.

"So Peng went out in the rain to find something. He came to a breadfruit tree and when he looked up, he saw a nice, big roaster. And as he was looking at it the ripe breadfruit fell right on his head!"

The four domino players laughed uproariously, and some of the other customers in the shop joined in the mirth.

"Good thing the breadfruit was well ripe," Papa continued, "or Peng would be a goner. The poto-poto from the breadfruit cover his head and face, nearly blind him. He had to scrape it off and feel his way down to the river to wash it off. Fortunately, he is fine."

7

"Him find any food?" asked Maas Kenny.

"Yes, he found a couple youngish breadfruits and took them home," continued Papa. "Miss Mirrie nearly died laughing when he told her about it. You can imagine her high-pitched laugh. She said such a thing would happen only to Peng."

"In all my born days is the first I ever hear something like that," said Maas Kenny. "Parson's wife from England asked me if coconuts fall on our heads. Said she saw it in a film show. I told her I never heard of it. Neither coconut nor breadfruit."

"Well, you hear about it now," said Papa.

Ossie bought the items his mother had sent him for – bulla cakes, cheese and sugar – and set off for home. He had seen Maas Peng and his wife a few times, but he had never spoken to either of them. Maas Peng was of medium height and had light-brown skin and curly hair. He was a carpenter and Ossie had seen him walking on the main road with his toolbox on his left shoulder. He had seen his wife a couple of times at Miss Lyn's shop. She was a small, thin woman with a resigned, fatalistic look in her eyes, and it was rumoured that she had a sharp tongue. Ossie had never heard of their having any children.

One day Ossie was sitting at the table having lunch with his father, when they heard a man's voice calling from the front of the house.

"Maas Johnny come quick! Landslide cover Maas Peng on Two Hills Road! Bring your shovel!"

"Coming!" replied Maas Johnny as he sprang from his chair, leaving his unfinished lunch. Ossie could hear him pulling his shovel from under the house. In a few moments he was with Papa in the yard. Ossie left his lunch and ran after them.

"Can I come?" he called.

"Yes, come," said his father.

They soon caught up with some other men who were hurrying along the main road. Most had hoes or shovels on their shoulders. From their conversations Ossie soon gathered that the recent rains had softened the soil, and had caused a large landslide to cover the road. A few people in the square recalled that Maas Peng, who had just spoken with them, had set off on the road on his way to the Post

8

Office. When news of the landslide spread, people began inquiring if anyone had seen Maas Peng. No one on either side of the landslide had seen him. So they concluded that the landslide had covered him. Men were already digging when they arrived.

"We have to be careful not to hurt him," Maas Johnny reminded them.

"Mek we keep calling out his name so he can hear us," suggested Papa.

"Peng! Peng! Maas Peng we coming!" they began chanting. "We coming, Peng!"

"I see his foot!" yelled Maas Kenny some minutes later.

A cheer went up.

They carefully removed the soil and hauled Maas Peng out of the earth.

"Him still alive!" said one of the men rejoicing.

"Unconscious but still alive," said Maas Johnny.

A woman who lived nearby was ready with a bucket of water, and she began splashing it on Maas Peng's face. After a few moments he opened his eyes. Another cheer went up. Maas Peng sputtered, and with the help of the men he sat up.

"How you feel, Maas Peng? How you feel?" asked Maas Johnny.

"Field? Field?" muttered Maas Peng. "Me field inna bush to rhatid, can't get anybody to help me weed it."

There was laughter at Maas Peng's misunderstanding.

"'Feel' Maas Peng, not 'field'," said one of the men.

"Feel? Feel?" said Maas Peng. "How would you feel if a blasted landslide came down on you?"

There was more laughter. The men were now engaging in lively banter with Maas Peng. Before long he was standing up. It appeared there were no broken bones. Some of the men escorted him home and his wife put him to bed. At Teacher Kerr's advice they took him to see a doctor the following day.

"Traumatized but otherwise fine," was the doctor's verdict.

The next time Maas Peng went to Maas Thom's bar, all the men bought him a drink. Papa rose from his stool, his slight paunch curved and smooth under his knitted shirt, and proposed a toast.

"To Maas Peng!" he said. "The ancients had their Jonah who came out of the belly of the whale. We have our Maas Peng who came out of the bowels of a landslide. We welcome him back to the land of the living. Be kind to Maas Peng. But there is one thing you must never do. Never ask him: How do you feel?"

Maas Peng joined in the laughter.

Some weeks later, Ossie overheard his father telling his mother another story about Maas Peng. His mother was at the sink washing dishes, and his father was in the yard attaching a stick to a new hoe. Ossie was in the dining room having a late Saturday-morning breakfast. He put together the story his father told.

Maas Peng and some other carpenters, including Maas Johnny, were building a house in a neighbouring district. On his way home from work one evening, Maas Peng stopped at Maas Thom's bar for a drink. He put down his toolbox at the door and went inside. Maas Thom, who had come to the district from China, ran the most highly regarded shop for miles around.

Maas Peng ordered a Q-Q (quarter quart) of white rum. Maas Thom knew the drinking habits of his customers, so he served Maas Peng his usual rum and water. Maas Thom was a reserved man with quiet, scholarly eyes, and it was rumoured that he used to be a university professor in China. From his conversations, Maas Peng associated him with fields of beans and barley, haystacks, piles of grain and statues of the Buddha. Maas Thom became agitated only when he denounced communism and Japanese aggression. Now as he drank, Maas Peng gradually guided the conversation to China, Maas Thom's favourite topic. Maas Thom began telling him about Chinese art, and that China was one of the few countries in the world where original works of art could be found in nearly every home.

Other men began entering the bar, and they began buying rounds of drinks. They began arguing about the usual topics: politics, crops, and the prices of produce. As twilight fell, some began leaving for supper at their homes. But Maas Peng ordered more liquor.

"Peng, you not going home to Miss Mirrie?" asked Maas Kenny.

"If young gal know what old wives know, dem would never wed," replied Maas Peng.

When Maas Peng began getting hungry, he ordered a red herring. Maas Thom lit a newspaper and roasted it right in front of him. Then he served it on a large, oval plate with slices of harddough bread. Maas Peng began devouring the food. Maas Thom offered him some Chinese tea, on the house, and Maas Peng gladly accepted the hot beverage. The tea was served in small porcelain cups, and Maas Thom explained that the absence of handles was so that they could warm people's palms in the winter.

More men arrived, and the drinking, arguing and storytelling continued into the night. Maas Thom kept moving from the bar to the shop as he manned both places. His wife was back in China, and he asked to be excused as he went to the back of the shop to prepare his dinner. The bar was full of the wonderful aroma of his cooking. The meal over, he rejoined the men. He listened as they debated, and seldom joined the discussion unless he was asked a specific question.

The men began going home. Although he tried not to show it, Maas Thom was getting tired and sleepy. He and Maas Peng were now the last ones left in the bar.

"Maas Thom, may I sleep in your bar tonight?" asked Maas Peng.

Maas Thom hesitated for a moment, and then said, "Sure." Except for inquiring about their children, he rarely got involved in the private lives of his customers. He began locking up the shop. Maas Peng brought his toolbox inside. Maas Thom handed him a chair over the counter so he would be able to rest more comfortably. Maas Thom put out the light and both men went to sleep.

The following morning Maas Thom served Maas Peng some bread and tea. Maas Peng thanked him for the night's rest. Then he lifted his toolbox to his shoulder and set off for the workplace he had left the evening before. That morning he was the first to arrive on the job.

"A man must go home to his wife," said Ossie's mother when his father was finished telling the story. "What was he doing sleeping in a rum bar when he has his bed at home?"

"It seems he is really afraid of Mirrie," said Maas Johnny.

11

"But sleeping in a bar won't help," said Miss Ona.

A few evenings later, Ossie had his first conversation with Maas Peng. He was standing on the bank at their gate and hoisting a kite he had made from a cocoa leaf, coconut spines and banana string. It would be carried into the air by what Mr. Llewellyn had called the Northeast Trade Winds, and which were now blowing at his back. It was a nice spot from which to fly a kite. On his left was a big mountain which sloped to smaller and more distant ones. Their blues merged into the greens which were closer to him. Before him, in the direction in which he would be flying the kite, the blue-green hills circled towards the west. A big green hill which rose from the bank of the road, blocked the sunset. As he was about to hoist the kite, he saw Maas Peng coming down the road, with his toolbox on his left shoulder. He was walking slowly, and his legs seemed a bit unsteady under the heavy weight. Ossie noticed the expression on his face. It was that of a man who had looked at the face of death more than once. His eyes looked out at a dangerous and unpredictable world. And there was a pain in them that Ossie did not know or understand. But Maas Peng was going home to his wife that evening, and even earlier than usual.

"Little boy, you went to school today?" asked Maas Peng.

"Yes, sah."

"And what they teach you?"

"Proverbs, sah," said Ossie after a moment's quick thinking.

"Tell me one."

"When trouble come, it don't set like rain." It was the first one that came to his mind.

"True word, me boy. Gospel truth dat. Give your father a message for me. Remind him that my corn shelling is tonight, and I would like him to come."

"Yes, sah."

Ossie watched as Maas Peng turned the corner and disappeared. Ossie loved corn shellings. People from the district assembled at each other's homes to help in the shelling of the year's corn crop. They told stories, guessed riddles and sang. They also ate asham, a fine powder made from parched corn which was pounded in a mortar and sweetened with brown sugar. People sometimes choked badly when they ate it. Ossie hoped that Mrs. Peng would keep a glass of water close to Maas Peng, just in case.

LOSERS
&
FINDERS

Maas Johnny stared at Ossie across the dining table. It was a look that told Ossie he was about to be told something of great importance. He waited for the punch to land.

"Don't let me ever see you hopping a truck," his father said. "Yesterday I saw some boys doing it. It is dangerous. You could get killed."

"Yes, sah," replied Ossie.

"Yes sah, what? Yes, you going to hop a truck, or yes you not going to do it?"

"I am not going to hop any truck, sah."

But a few days later, on his way home from school in the company of his classmates Phonso, Washie and Brightly, they heard the sound of an automobile coming behind them.

"Sounds like Maas Vin's truck," said Phonso. "Mek we hop it."

"My legs tired so a ride would do me good," said Washie as he began running on the spot.

"That truck can't leave me!" said Brightly, his eyes showing the reason for his pet name.

14

Ossie said nothing but he felt his heart hammering. The sound of the truck was getting louder as it groaned and belched around the corners. Then the red cab appeared about a hundred yards from them. The boys moved to the side of the road and waited.

As soon as the truck passed them, Phonso chased it and threw his bag to someone on the back seat. Then he held on and climbed up into the vehicle. Washie and Brightly were now chasing after it.

"Come, Ossie!" Phonso shouted from the truck.

Ossie hesitated. Then he decided he wouldn't do it. There was a saying that even trees have eyes and ears, so word would probably get back to his father. Besides a little more walking would not kill him.

"Ossie, you are a sissy!" Phonso shouted from the truck.

Washie and Brightly were now climbing into the vehicle. Ossie saw the men on the back- seat laughing at him. The truck was moving away rapidly. Safe on the back- seat, Washie and Brightly joined Phonso in urging him on.

"Come on Ossie! Come on Ossie!" they shouted.

Sissy indeed! thought Ossie. I will show them! He began chasing the truck, with his friends encouraging him. He got to it just as it slowed down to negotiate a bend. He held up his small suitcase and one of the men grabbed it. Then he held on to the truck and found a grip for his feet. He felt the firm hand of one of the men on his arm. They hauled him into the truck and helped him to a seat. Then he noticed a car close behind the truck. What if he had fallen?

"Attaboy Ossie!" said Phonso.

"I thought I told you not to hop trucks!" said Ossie's father from one of the seats behind Ossie. Ossie could not believe his ears, but when he turned he saw that he was not hallucinating. His father was glaring at him from two rows up.

"Cho Maas Johnny!" said one of the women. "Give the boy a chance. Boys will be boys."

"Chance? Wait till we get home!"

Ossie knew he was in trouble. He envied Phonso who did not know who his father was. Washie's father spent most of the year as a farmworker in the States. Brightly's father beat him only when he

15

was drunk. But his father was very sober and clear-eyed about beatings. It seemed the journey to the village square took only a few minutes. His father's face was stony as they climbed down from the truck. And his father remained silent as they began walking side by side towards their gate.

"How was I supposed to know you would be on the truck?" complained Ossie.

"Good thing I had to go down to Evansville to buy some nails and bolts. Otherwise I wouldn't know you are a truck-hopper."

"It was the first time I hop a truck."

"And I am going to make sure it is the last. Wait till we get home!"

As soon as they got to the yard, Ossie saw his father unbuckling his belt. He braced himself for a beating. But as soon as the leather belt was swinging in his father's hand, Ossie's mother rushed out of the house and grabbed it.

"Don't beat him!" she begged. "Is what him do?"

"Hop truck. Even though I warned him."

"But at least he didn't harm himself. And he won't do it again. Go inside, Ossie!"

Ossie ran into his room.

It was a grim and silent supper. After his mother cleared away the dishes, Ossie had the table to himself to do his homework. It was then that he missed his pen. He searched his pickets and his suitcase, but it was nowhere to be found. The pen was a gift from his Uncle Basil, a sergeant in The Royal Air Force. He had an interest in Ossie's education, and did everything he could to encourage him. He had bought the pen in Malta, and had given it to Ossie on one of his holiday visits home. To lose it would be a tragedy, thought Ossie. He was in an agony of spirit.

"I lost Uncle Basil's pen," he wailed to his mother as she was putting dishes in the cabinet.

"Dropped it while hopping the truck, no doubt," said his father who had just entered the dining room, and was waiting to take something from the drawer of the cabinet.

"Ask Teacher Kerr to announce it at devotion," suggested his mother.

The following morning Ossie told the headmaster about the loss of his pen. The school went through the morning devotions in the usual way, with the children standing in their classrooms as Mr. Kerr took them through the singing, Bible reading and prayers. Then he made the announcement in his big, strong voice. The loss of Ossie's pen was the last item on his list. Then he added:

"That pen was brought here all the way from Malta. Do you know where Malta is? It is an island in the Mediterranean Sea, so called because the people who lived around it in olden days thought it was the middle of the world. But many great civilizations sprang up around it, including Greece and Rome. And that is where this pen came from, only to be lost. It is a blue pen with a silver top. So if you find it please return it to Oswald Johnson who is the rightful owner, or bring it to me."

Ossie was pleased about the announcement, and he began praying that someone would find and return his pen.

It was a time of drought, and it was one of Ossie's duties to rise early and fetch water from one of the village tanks. This tank was legendary for its faithfulness, for although it offered a mere drip during times of drought, even the oldest people in the district could not remember a time when it dried up completely. It was still dark when Ossie set off with his zinc pan. He crossed the main road and began following a path downhill towards the valley. He soon discovered that the white dress moving in front of him was Paulette's, and that she was carrying a pail in her right hand.

"I like the early morning," she said, "for we may find some rounie mangoes."

"I like them," said Ossie, "they are very sweet."

The rounie mango tree was on the hillside on their right, but it was on Mr. Stuart's property. He owned fierce dogs. He also owned a bus, a truck and a car, and was the richest man in the district. But not even his fierce dogs could prevent the mangoes from falling and rolling down to the path. Ossie and Paulette were lucky that morning, for it seemed they were the first to arrive under the tree and they found several of the prized fruits waiting for them.

"You go first," said Ossie when they got to the tank.

They listened as the water trickled into Paulette's pail. It would take a long time to fill the containers, so they sat on a concrete slab and waited.

"I know who has your pen," said Paulette.

"Who?"

"Mrs. Wilson, the postmistress. Her daughter found it."

"Who told you?"

"Is so me hear. Mrs. Wilson wants you to come to her and ask for it."

That evening Ossie stopped at the Postal Agency on his way home from school. Mrs. Wilson was a fat, dark-skinned woman with a loud voice, who loved to tell jokes and laugh. When Ossie arrived at the window she was slotting letters into the boxes.

"Good evening, son," she said as she turned and glanced at him. "No letters for your parents today."

Ossie hesitated, then he ventured an inquiry: "I am here about the pen, mam."

"Pen? Which pen?"

"I lost my pen, mam."

Mrs. Wilson paused and turned to look at him. She gave him a penetrating stare. He had seldom seen her face look so serious.

"Describe the pen," she said. Ossie described it as best as he could.

"Where did you lose it?"

Ossie mentioned the spot where he had hopped the truck. Mrs. Wilson reached over and pulled the pen from a jar on the table. She held it up before him.

"Is this the pen?"

"Yes, mam!" said Ossie overjoyed at the sight of his pen.

"You must take better care of your pen," she said as she handed it to him. "And I hear it came all the way from Malta."

"Yes, mam. Uncle Basil has been to many places, including places in the Bible like Jerusalem and Bethlehem."

"As a child I believed those places were in heaven!" she said with a laugh.

"Thank you very much, mam," said Ossie.

"You're welcome."

"Bye Mrs. Wilson."

"Bye Ossie."

At supper that evening, a smiling Ossie showed his parents the recovered pen, and told them about Mrs. Wilson.

"Bless Mrs. Wilson," said his mother. "She is not one of those persons who believe that finders should be keepers."

"Uncle Basil will forgive you now," said his father.

"He is smiling wherever he is," said his mother. "In Nazareth or Singapore."

On his way to the tank the following morning, Ossie met Paulette coming up the path with her pail on her head.

"I found two rounies. You want one?" She held out her hand with the mangoes.

"Thanks," said Ossie as he took one of the fruits. "I got back my pen. Thank you for telling me."

"I am glad. Especially since it seemed to be such a special pen."

"It would have been hard living with myself knowing that I lost Uncle Basil's pen."

"He seems like a very kind man."

"Very kind."

"Bye, Ossie. Hurry up. Seems as if you overslept this morning. Too glad to get back your pen!"

Ossie chuckled and began running down the path.

At school that morning he reported to Teacher Kerr that he had recovered his pen.

"Good," said the headmaster, with a rare, soft look on his face. "Now write some good compositions with it."

"I will try, Sir," replied Ossie.

With his pen safe in his breast pocket, Ossie relaxed and listened as Mrs. Roberts, his chubby, brown Sunday school teacher, told them the story of The Feeding of the Five Thousand. She read from the Bible about how Jesus fed a multitude with five loaves and two fishes. He loved the stories about miracles, and this was his favourite. It was the one he would most like to be present at. He had tasted the wine from one of his mother's bottles and he didn't care for it, so they could keep the turning of water into wine. But bread and fish was one of his favourite combinations. His mother bought fish from a van that passed through the district from time to time, and she fried them in coconut oil with vinegar, onions and peppers; when combined with freshly baked harddough bread, this was as close to paradise as he could imagine. Yet, from what Mrs. Roberts was saying, the bread and fish produced by Jesus must have tasted even better. She showed them pictures from a colour book. Those loaves were round, not long and thick like most of those he was accustomed to. But round breads were especially prized in the district, especially on Christmas morning. So Ossie wondered if those round breads were inspired by those of Bible days, and if there was some special religious significance in their shape.

The memory of the miracle of the loaves and fishes was still in his mind when Vincent Chen's blue-grey bread van passed him on the main road one morning. The aroma of the breads, buns and cakes filled the air, tinged only with the scent of smoke from the van's muffler. With the exception of the scent of mangoes, no other aroma delighted him more than that of freshly baked bread. He felt himself fantasizing that the door of the van would fly open and that all the baked goods would be hurled in front of him. But the van turned the corner, and he could hear it as it headed for Maas Thom's shop.

Vincent Chen almost always wore white shirts and grey trousers, and his polished black shoes, that seemed unusually small to Ossie, glistened in the sunshine. His delivery route took him through the district once per week. But sometimes he came back on weekends, for he was courting Dawn, Mr. Stuart's pretty brown daughter.

For years after, Ossie would marvel at the event which occurred a few weeks later. It was during the holidays, and his mother served what was, even by her usual high standards, a remarkable lunch. It was susumber, saltfish, and tomatoes cooked in coconut run-down, with yellow yam, sweet potatoes and boiled green bananas. After devouring it, he washed it down with sour-orange-ade sweetened with wet sugar, and chilled with chunks of ice. His stomach was so full he was reminded of his father's words, for if his mother asked him to do something while he was hungry he would say, "Empty bag can't stand up"; and if she asked him after a meal he would joke, "And full bag can't bend". Ossie felt he was too full to bend, but unlike him, his rabbits and guinea-pigs were hungry, so he set off to get some feeding for them.

He was walking on the main road when he heard the unmistakable sound of Vincent Chen's bread van approaching behind him. He stepped out of the way to let it pass. It left the usual aroma of baked goods in its wake, and he enjoyed it, but he was too full to indulge in his fantasy that day. The door of the van suddenly flew open, and breads, buns and cakes tumbled out. In an instant an abundance of food was scattered over the road. Vincent Chen was obviously unaware of what had happened, for the van continued driving up the road.

Seeming to appear out of thin air, people descended on the food. An old woman converted the front of her dress into a container and was piling loaves into it. "Thank God fi Jesus!" she exclaimed. "Food deh pan table tonight!" Phonso, who was nowhere to be seen a moment before, was now chewing a spice bun and stuffing bulla cakes into his pockets. People were climbing down the bank and coming up from the bushes. "Is like manna fall from the sky!" said a man as he dismounted from his donkey.

Ossie remained motionless. Was this a case of the mind over matter that Mr. Llewellyn liked to talk about? Was this The Feeding of the One Hundred? He had yearned for this moment and now it was right in front of him. So he felt he should at least say thank you to it. His eyes fell on a spice bun that Phonso had not yet gotten to and he moved towards it.

"Ossie!" It was his mother's voice behind him, and he turned to see her coming up the road with her basket in her hand.

"Stop there this minute!" she commanded. "Did you give Mr. Chen anything to put down? Leave the man's things alone!" Ossie stopped in his tracks.

At that moment Vincent Chen swung around the corner walking with long strides. People began to scatter. Some went over the bank. Others went up and down the road, with bowed heads or averted eyes. A few remained standing, caught in the act of eating, with self-conscious smiles and grins on their faces. Vincent Chen surveyed the scene, with a slight suggestion of pain in his eyes. The people waited for him to say something.

"No matter where you go, there you are," he said.

Ossie wondered what he meant. People said he was only the driver of the van, not the owner of the bakery. Perhaps the lost money would be deducted from his salary. This was an irretrievable loss on his part. Mr. Chen turned and began walking back to his van. And Ossie felt very sorry for him.

THE HARVEST FESTIVAL

Mr. Llewellyn taught all subjects. He also sang solos at school concerts, and was the best whistler Ossie had ever heard, for he could whistle more than one part of a song at the same time. It was reported that he was also a good tailor and shoemaker. On a visit to his home, Ossie had once seen him ironing his trousers on an iron board, and using one of the old time internally heating coal irons that tailors used. So it was not surprising that handicrafts were one of his favourite subjects. One Monday morning he announced that he would teach the class how to make baskets. On the coming Friday they should take bundles of coconut spines and leaves to school.

Ossie explored their farm in search of fallen coconut boughs, and he found two that had green and yellow leaves. He used his penknife to remove the leaves and get to the spines. He assembled the spines into a bundle and tied it with a piece of banana string. Then he made another bundle from the strips of leaves. When Friday morning came he set off for school with his raw materials.

After the roll-call Mr. Llewellyn began his lesson. Displaying the artistic skills that he also possessed, he drew diagrams on the blackboard showing the sequence to be followed. First, the spines were to be assembled in bundles of ten and wrapped with strips of leaves. Second, the bundles were to be wrapped and bent into rings. Third, five rings were to be assembled to form the bottom and four sides of the basket. Fourth, the spines would be netted to fill in the spaces in the rings. Finally, the spines of the two smaller rings which faced each other would be brought together at the top until they overlapped; they would then be wrapped with strips of leaves to form the handle of the basket.

The class was a hum of concentrated activity as the pupils worked. There was never any corporal punishment during handicrafts, for the pupils were too busy to get into trouble. Ossie worked and was pleased to see his basket taking shape in his hands. By lunch time the pupils were all finished and having a good time showing off their handiwork to each other.

Ossie's mother was sitting on the verandah sewing when he arrived home that afternoon.

"What a pretty basket!" she said when he showed it to her. "You really made it fi true?"

"Yes."

"You can enter it in the Harvest Festival Basket Competition."

"I didn't remember about it."

"And the Famitry Band will be playing."

"What is the Famitry Band?"

"It really should be The Reformatory Band, but people call it that for short."

"What is a reformatory?"

"A school where they send bad boys. Where you may end up if you don't watch yourself."

"And they have their own band?"

"Yes. The government believes that playing music can help to cure them."

Ossie decided to enter the competition. During the week preceding the event, he began collecting produce for his basket. He secured an avocado pear, three oranges, a grapefruit and some cucumbers. But he wasn't satisfied with a plain basket, so he decorated it with strips of coloured kite paper. He thought his creation was very beautiful, almost like something for a wedding.

On the Sunday afternoon of the function, Ossie set off for the church, dressed in a white shirt, blue necktie and matching pants, and black shoes that shone. Several persons stopped him on the road to admire and praise his basket. Their praise was so spontaneous and lavish he began to entertain the thought that he might actually win the competition.

When he entered the churchyard he saw some of his friends standing under the Poinciana tree.

"That is definitely the first prize," said Phonso.

"I don't have anything to hand in," said Washie, "but my mother brought some eggs."

"Remember to render your hearts and not your garments," said Brightly.

While they were chatting, the bus with the Famitry Band arrived. The boys made a striking picture in their blue uniforms with silver trim. They carried their instruments in cases. Maas Ishy, a deacon of the church, came out to meet them. He wore a pin-striped blue suit, and his paunch was so big it was rumoured that he could not see his feet. He shook hands with the band leader, a strapping man in a khaki military uniform, and hailed and welcomed the boys. Then he led them up the steps towards the vestry. Members of the congregation who had been waiting and conversing in the yard now began entering the building.

When Ossie and his friends entered the church the delightful market-like aroma of the donated produce hit their nostrils. Maas Ishy's much discussed gift of a complete banana tree, with its bunch of fruit and all, was tied to one of the columns. Choice stalks of various species of sugar cane, with their leaves intact, were tied to the other columns, and formed a colonnade alongside the benches. At the base of one of the columns was a now famous 120-lb yam, a gift from Maas Peng and his wife; people were gathered around it and admiring and discussing it, with some saying it was a miracle. A newspaper article had been published about it. With the heavy aroma of the produce in their nostrils, which was a contrast to that of the camphor balls and washed and ironed fabrics they were accustomed to, the boys took their seats in the children's section on the left. The church was used as a school on weekdays, and Ossie was able to rest his basket on the wooden desk in front of him which pupils used mostly for reading and writing. The church was rapidly filling up with worshippers.

The Famitry Band was now sitting on the platform where the choir usually sat. Their instruments were out of their cases and they glistened and shone. Ossie was excited by the amazing shapes and colours of the instruments, especially those made of brass. Combined with the blue and silver uniforms, the band made an impressive picture.

The Rev. Peter Johnson, the minister of the church, emerged from the vestry and mounted the pulpit. He was a brown man with curly hair, and he wore rimless spectacles. In a voice with the rhythms and cadences Ossie had only heard from parsons, he announced the opening hymn: "We plough the fields and scatter." The choir, dressed in white, and now seated at front-right, rose to lead the singing, accompanied by Mrs. Roberts on the organ. The rest of the congregation rose to join them.

After the hymn and the opening prayer, the minister welcomed everyone, especially the Famitry Band who had come, he said, to help them make a joyful noise unto the Lord.

"Thank you for bringing the produce of your farms to the house of the Lord," he continued. "As the great poet John Milton said, 'God doth not need either man's work or his own gifts'. But by giving we take a step towards transforming ourselves for his glory."

The service progressed, and soon it was time for the children's presentation of gifts. Ossie joined the line. When it was his turn he recited the Bible verse that he had chosen as his quotation: "Remember now thy Creator in the days of thy youth, while the evil days come not nor the years draw nigh, when thou shalt say, I have no pleasure in them. Ecclesiastes 12:1." The minister thanked him, took the basket, and then placed his hand on Ossie's head and blessed him. Ossie returned to his seat.

There were more hymns and Bible readings. The offering was taken. Then it was time for the band to play. The tall band leader faced the congregation and announced the titles of the pieces. Then he turned and signalled the start of the music. Ossie watched his floating arms as he conducted the band. The shining instruments came alive as each declared its identity. The church was full of rich and wonderful sounds. It was quite a contrast to the often out of tune singing that Ossie was used to hearing there. He was very impressed by a saxophonist, a boy of his own age. The boy stood with legs apart, in a boasy stance, and with puffed cheeks he belted out the sounds so dramatically there were periodic bursts of applause from the audience. Ossie wondered what he had done to be placed in a reformatory. But with the music he was playing, it seemed he was definitely cured.

With the solo over, the boy bowed in gratitude to the applauding congregation. The band then played some of the British music Ossie had heard on Maas Thom's radio. This was followed by some Jamaican folksongs he recognized, including "Mango Time", "Banana" and "Evening Time". The band brought the set to an end and received enthusiastic applause.

There was another hymn. Then the minister preached a sermon on The Parable of the Sower. The thoughts were beautiful and inspiring, Ossie thought, but he found himself wishing they would get on with the judging of the baskets. At the end of what seemed like a very long sermon, the minister announced that the judging would begin during the singing of the next hymn, and would continue during the musical interlude. Mrs. Roberts would be the chief judge and she would be assisted by two other teachers from the school.

During the hymn Ossie watched as the three women examined the baskets. They had clipboards and they made notes as they examined each entry. Ossie noticed that they paused for a long time over his basket. After the hymn the congregation sat and the band struck up the folksong "Hallelujah", followed by "What a Wonderful Thing". The judges began to confer. When their minds were made up, they signalled to the minister that they were ready to announce the results. Mrs. Roberts mounted the platform and faced the audience.

"Ladies and gentlemen, boys and girls," she said. "First of all we would like to congratulate all the children who entered this competition. We are sure that in the eyes of the Lord they are all winners. But we would like to mention three of them who, in our eyes, are artistically outstanding. So third place goes to Oswald Johnson!"

Ossie's heart sank. He had felt sure he would have gotten first place. He heard the mocking laughter of the boys behind him.

"Ossie crash!" said one of them.

"If only three had entered, Ossie would have come last," said Phonso.

"We would like to commend Oswald," continued Mrs. Roberts. "His basket was very original, for we have never seen one like it before. He also had a fine selection of produce. But we think that his basket is over-decorated. It doesn't need all that fancy paper. By itself, it would have been fine."

"Second place goes to Annette Reid. She has a nice old time basket, and we especially admired the beautiful design she created with the soursop and the ackee.

"And now, we come to the big winner, the first place. She had, not a basket, but a tray of very artistically arranged fruits and vegetables. She let the beauty of the items speak for themselves. The design is simple, unified and strong. Congratulations to Paulette Wedderburn!"

While the congregation applauded, Mrs. Roberts walked elegantly back to her seat at the organ.

Ossie observed the flutter of excitement in the front row as the other girls reached over to congratulate Paulette. Her curls shook as she turned from right to left to acknowledge the congratulations. Ossie was happy that Paulette had won. If not me, then Paulette, he said to himself.

The minister returned to the pulpit and congratulated the winners. He endorsed Mrs. Roberts's view that all the children were winners, for, he said, Jesus suffered all the little children to come unto him. Then he announced that the band would play the final set.

The band launched into some very rousing marches. There was one that made Ossie feel like getting up and marching left right, left right. At the same time, he found the tune beautiful and haunting. He found himself tapping his toes to its rhythm.

28

The minister announced that the sale of the gifts would be the following day, and he urged the congregation to give it their full support. He said the proceeds would be for the church's building fund and for poor relief. Then he gave the vote of thanks to all, including those who had given gifts, the officers of the church, and the band that had brought "wonderful refreshment for the spirit". Then he invited the congregation to stand for the final hymn. After this he gave the benediction. Several persons moved forward to take a closer look at the baskets, and especially at the winners which were now placed together. Others began leaving the building. Ossie went to the front and congratulated Paulette and Annette.

"Ossie, you should have won," said Paulette.

"No, the judges know best," replied Ossie.

"I am glad that Clifton got two of the top three places. We should celebrate!"

They saw Mrs. Roberts approaching them.

"Congratulations Paulette, Annette and Ossie," she said. "Ossie where did you get that basket?"

Ossie told her about Mr. Llewelyn.

"I have given notice that I will be buying it tomorrow," continued Mrs. Roberts. "You can make another for your mother. In fact, I think you should make them and sell them. Earn some pocket money."

"Thanks mam," said Ossie.

Ossie went outside hoping to catch up with his friends, but they were nowhere to be seen. Most people were rushing home. Ossie found himself walking alongside the young saxophonist.

"Boy, you really know how to play that thing," said Ossie.

"Thank you," said the boy, turning to him.

"What is the name of this one?" Ossie began humming his favourite march.

"Semper Fidelis," the boy replied.

"What does it mean?"

"Faithful Always. It was composed by John Phillip Sousa."

"I like it very much."

"Thanks. Bye," said the boy as he began walking towards the bus.

Ossie stood and watched as the band boarded the bus. Maas Ishy was with them, and he shook hands with the leader and waved to the boys. As soon as they were all inside, the engine started and the bus, which had been put into a departure position during the service, began leaving the churchyard slowly. Ossie watched until it disappeared, taking the boys to the mysterious life of the reformatory.

"Well done, son," said his mother as she approached him in the company of one of her church sisters.

"Thanks," replied Ossie.

"If he does his other school work as well as he makes baskets, he will do well," the other woman said to Ossie's mother.

"He is a hard worker," said his mother.

"Bye," said Ossie as he left them and began hurrying, hoping to catch up with his friends. But they had all disappeared.

At home his mother served cassava pudding, cheese and mint tea for supper.

"Ossie came third with his basket," she told Maas Johnny.

"Why didn't he come first?" he replied.

"Third not bad," said Miss Ona. "Most never made it to the top three. And winning is not all. He made a contribution."

Maas Johnny sipped his tea but said nothing. But Ossie thought he saw a little glimmer of pride in his eyes. Ossie and his father remained silent as Miss Ona recapped some of the highlights of the service.

After supper Ossie sat on the steps to the dining room and played his bamboo fife. After a few attempts he managed to play Semper Fidelis. He noticed that the notes were clean, simple and strong. Perhaps they were like the fruits and vegetables on Paulette's tray, he thought.

THE MONGOOSE

Ossie was fascinated by the animals around him. Once, he dug up an ants nest and put it into a bottle so he could watch as the clever animals reconstructed it. One night while he was studying at the dining table a mouse crept up to his books. He put food in a brown paper bag as bait and trapped it. He let it go, but this gave him an idea to trap one and keep it as a pet. Using his father's tools, he converted a wooden box he found under the house into a cage. He placed a sheet of glass on top so he could see inside. Then he caught a mouse and put it inside. But when he returned from school the following evening he found that the mouse had cut a beautiful round hole through the side of the box and had escaped. Another night while he was studying, a huge buzzing insect flew in through the window. It had a single bright light on its forehead, not two like the peeny-wallies he was used to, and it began circling the lamp with great vigour. He had a difficult time getting it out of the house. But it made him wonder if there were many such unidentified monsters in the woodlands. He loved the birds most of all, and there was an abundance of them. His favourites included the robin redbreasts who bore holes on banks to make their nests.

Woodpeckers were another favourite, and he wondered if they got headaches from hammering the trunks of trees with their beaks. His mother feared the green and croaking lizards that crawled on the trees and sometimes came into the house, but he was indifferent to them. The main animal he encountered in the bushes was the mongoose.

He was surrounded by fascinating plants, fruit-trees like mangoes, star apples, custard apples, rose apples and jackfruits. His father cultivated yams, sweet potatoes and bananas. His mother planted tomatoes, cabbages and cucumbers. His mother planted a beautiful garden in front of the house, and was very devoted to it. His father expressed his domesticity mostly by pruning the hibiscus hedge. He never allowed the leaves to grow very high, and the constant pruning caused them to spread out and form what looked like a thick mat. Ossie's contribution to this domestic scene was to collect wild orchids and plant them in coconut husks; he hung them on the mango tree beside his mother's garden.

Ossie included some of these things in an essay entitled "Wildlife in my District" that Mr. Llewellyn had given the class as homework one weekend. Phonso wrote about rum-drinking, gambling and fighting, and became the butt of jokes when Mr. Llewelyn explained what he meant by "Wildlife". Then he read Ossie's essay to the class.

"I think Oswald is going to become a naturalist," he said when he was finished reading.

"What is a naturalist, Sir?" asked Ossie.

"Someone who studies the objects in nature, especially in their natural state. This is called natural history. It includes subjects like biology, botany and zoology. You will learn more about those later in your education."

One morning Ossie was in the front yard trying out a gig he had just carved from the wood of a guava tree. He watched with satisfaction as the top was spinning smoothly on the ground. He was ready for the gig season and the pecking contests with Phonso, Washie and Brightly. He heard the chickens squawking and cackling with great agitation.

"Mongoose! Mongoose!" he heard his mother calling. "Mongoose!"

He picked up his gig and rushed to see what was happening. The chickens were rushing up from the bushes into the yard. His mother was throwing cracked corn to them and chanting, "Coop! Coop! Coop!"

"It look like the mongoose t'ief one of mi fowl," she said. "Mi best layer. T'iefing mongoose!"

By the evening it was confirmed. Ossie overheard his mother telling his father about the missing chicken. He heard the sound of distress in his mother's voice.

"Watch me and him," said his father. "You just watch me and him!"

That night while lying in bed Ossie thought about the mongoose. He remembered that he and his dog Chewy had chased one to its hole in the culvert's gully. Chewy had dug vigorously and he had gone back to the house to get his father's digging-bill. But in spite of all their efforts they never got to the mongoose, for it seemed its nest was very deep or it had escaped through another exit.

He knew that mongooses were reputed to be very daring, for according to a proverb, "Mongoose seh: If you don't take chance yuh no man". They took chances by raiding chicken yards, sometimes in full view of the occupants.

It was also believed that they could be signs of good or ill fortune. If one crossed the road in front of you it was a sign of good fortune. You would succeed on your mission. But if he got to the middle of the road and then turned back, this indicated ill fortune. You could expect disappointment, so you might want to turn back.

It was after lunch, and with the roll call completed, Mr. Llewellyn prepared for his geography lesson. He hung a map of the world on the blackboard. They would be learning some of the capital cities of the world. But before he could begin, Ossie raised his hand.

"Sir, please tell us about the mongoose."

The class tittered, and some of the girls in the front now turned to look at Ossie. "What Ossie want to know about mongoose?" asked Paulette.

Mr. Llewelyn raised his hand to his chin and looked very thoughtful for a few moments. Then he spoke:

"The mongoose was brought to Jamaica from India to kill rats and snakes in the cane fields. They were very successful with the snakes, for those are seldom seen on the island nowadays. But the rats are still very much with us. The mongoose nearly wiped out the iguanas as well. But since they had no natural enemies they multiplied and became pests. They are now a scourge to people who raise chickens."

Then Mr. Llewellyn burst into song and gave a spirited rendition of "Sly Mongoose".

"Mongoose go inna Bedward kitchen
Pluck weh one a him righteous chicken
Put it inna him waistcoat pocket
Sly mongoose!
Mongoose say him a Bedward member
Bedward say him nuh quite remember
Mongoose say him join last December
Sly mongoose!"

Mr. Llewelyn took down the map and wrote the words of the song on the blackboard. "Sing with me!" he said, and the class joined in. Then he explained that Alexander Bedward was a messianic Jamaican cult leader who promised that he would fly to heaven with his followers. The manifestation failed. He was arrested, tried, declared insane, and committed to the mental hospital where he remained until his death. The song is about a young man who succeeded in wooing away a young woman from Bedward's church.

"Now that you understand it, sing again!" said Mr. Llewelyn.

They sang so vigorously people from the other classes came to peep at what was happening. Mr. Llewelyn erased the song and mounted his map a second time. He began telling them about Kingston, the capital of Jamaica, a city in which mongooses can sometimes be seen in gardens.

The following morning, as he was about to leave for school, Ossie saw his father making a mongoose trap. It was a wooden box made of sticks which allowed one to see inside. His father explained that if the mongoose entered to get the bait – which would be a piece of meat – it would agitate the string and cause the door to fall and trap it inside. He would place the trap on a stretch of level land near the house.

Ossie found it difficult to concentrate on his lessons. He kept wondering if the trap would catch the mongoose. Perhaps he would be too sly to go in.

He went home for lunch but before having his meal he went to look at the trap. Sure enough there was a mongoose inside! The animal was running to and fro, furiously trying to get out. Ossie felt sorry for the trapped creature. He remembered what Mr. Llewellyn had said about his being a budding naturalist, someone who studied animals in their wild state. Furthermore, he felt grateful to the mongoose for killing off most of the snakes, the animals he liked least. It was true he had never seen a live snake, and did not want to, even if it was said there were no poisonous ones on the island. He felt so grateful to the trapped mongoose that was trying so desperately to escape. What was his crime? Ossie wondered. He liked chicken meat. But so did most people, except that they preferred it fried, roasted or curried.

So he bent down and opened the door and let the mongoose out. In a flash it scurried across the grass and disappeared into the bushes. As he stood over the empty trap reflecting on what he had just done, he heard footsteps and saw his father coming down the path carrying a machete. His father stared at the empty trap.

"Where is the mongoose?" he demanded. "He was just there. I went for my machete."

"I let him out," said Ossie.

"Let him out!" yelled his father. "You mad or what, boy?" He glared at Ossie with blazing eyes.

"What kind of idiot do I have for a son? If the mongoose eats our chickens where will we get meat to eat? Where will we get eggs to sell to buy your clothes and books? Look here, boy. I am going to reset that trap. And if you let him out again," he looked up at the heavens prayerfully, "the police going to have to come for me because of you!"

Ossie lost his appetite and had to force himself to have some of his lunch. He returned to school with a heavy heart. The geography lesson seemed tiresome. His ears pricked up only when Mr. Llewellyn mentioned New Delhi, the capital of India.

India. That was where the mongoose came from. He wondered how they were doing over there.

"Your father caught the mongoose," his mother said when he returned home that evening. "Or perhaps it is another one. But I don't think so. They are very persistent and don't give up easily."

"And he killed him," declared Ossie.

"Yes."

Ossie said nothing. He went into his room to change his clothes. He told himself there was probably nothing he could do to prevent people from killing mongooses. When he was dressed he went out to the verandah where his mother was sitting and sewing. He walked out into the yard.

"Where you going?" asked his mother.

"To play gig with my friends," he replied.

THE GAMBLER

O ssie's mother and father enjoyed their dinner of cowfoot, rice and peas and raw tomatoes sprinkled with coconut oil. But Ossie did not like the gluey cowfoot, so he ate very little. By nightfall he began feeling hungry. He recalled that he had just enough pocket money to buy a single bulla cake, so he set off for Maas Thom's shop.

The dark night had come down very quickly, and it was now cool and pleasant. As he was leaving the yard he could smell the fragrance of jasmine coming from his mother's garden. He walked to the gate, turned right and began following the main road. It was a walk that made him think of food. But it was not mango season, so there were no ripe beefy mangoes on the road under the tree on his left. And there were no tamarinds on the tree on his right. But he could not help thinking about the delicious drink his mother made from this fruit. He loved it with chunks of ice, and foaming with the baking soda she put into it.

When he entered the square he saw a group of men gathered in front of a small table on the piazza. They were lit by a hurricane lantern on the floor beside the table. As Ossie approached he saw that the man behind the table wore a beret and dark glasses. Ossie wondered why he wore dark glasses in the night. The man was dealing cards on the table and bantering with his audience. Ossie noticed that he was gap toothed and spoke with a lisp.

Ossie joined the group and watched the game. The gambler shuffled a deck of cards, and then placed the top three face-down on the table, making sure his audience had a glimpse of their faces before he put them down. Then he called the name of one of the cards, and challenged the men to pick it up. If someone wanted to play, he placed a coin on the table and then picked up the card he thought was the correct one. If he was right his money was doubled. If he was wrong, he lost his bet. Ossie observed that some of the men were winning and some were losing.

"I think I figure out this thing, so you just watch me and him," said a tall man who, like the gambler, Ossie was seeing in the district for the first time.

The tall man started betting and scored a string of victories. He was just shoving money into his pocket. Encouraged by his success, other men began betting as well. Some won for a while. Then they began losing. After a while some went into the shop to complete their business. Some left for their homes.

"Youth man," said the gambler as his eyes fell on Ossie. "You want to take a chanth?"

Ossie thought about it for a few moments. If he lost with his first try his bulla cake would be gone. But if he won and won again he would be on his way to not only a cake but a slice of cheese as well. He could even make it to a tin of sardines. If he hit it big time, he could buy a tin of bully beef and some slices of bread. In a flashback he recalled that he had correctly identified the cards a few times. The gambler said, "Youth man, the Bible say, time and chance happeneth."

"Awright," said Ossie. The gambler shuffled the deck and Ossie saw him put down a Jack of Diamonds, an Ace of Spades and a Queen of Hearts.

"Jack!" said the gambler. Ossie picked up the Jack.

"Oi. Oi. Whoi!" wailed the gambler in mock pain. "De youth man lick me fi thix!"

He doubled Ossie's money. The feel of another coin in his hand gave Ossie a sense of success and power. Even more could be his, he told himself.

"Mith Matilda from Vineyard Town bought her firth lottery ticket," said the gambler. "Won five million dolla! Bought a little houth and a car. What you want to buy youth man?"

"A bicycle."

"Then pick the Queen of Spades!" he said after he had shuffled the deck and placed three cards down.

It was another victory for Ossie.

"Dith youth man wicked!" declared the gambler.

Ossie noticed that the tall man was smiling mysteriously. One of the men from the district smiled at Ossie and nodded. The gambler was shuffling the deck again.

"Dem cath lot in de Bible," he said, "tho why not cath it here? Youth man, cath your lot with me now. Pick the Ace of Diamonds!"

There was applause from the men when Ossie won again. Now he could almost taste the bully beef. The last time he had had it in the rough was with his friends when they "ran a boat" one Friday evening after school. He was getting hungrier and hungrier. And the money was growing in his pocket.

"You play cricket?" asked the gambler.

"Yeth ... I mean yes."

"Batsman or bowler?"

"Spin bowler."

"You the captain?"

"Vice captain for the Under Eleven Team."

"Tho imagine the captain thick, and you have to call the toth. Head or tail? Could make the difference if you win or lothe the game. Call Ace of Spades!"

This time Ossie lost his money. The defeat stung him. Was there something wrong with card games after all, as his mother believed? He had learnt to play some of them at social evenings put on by Mr. Llewellyn's scout troop, to which he belonged. But his mother wouldn't allow him to play cards with his friends and relatives in the house.

But if Mr. Llewelyn allowed them, what could be so wrong? he wondered.

"You have brothath and sithtahs?" asked the gambler.

"No."

"Which would you prefer?"

"A sister."

"Would you bet on it?"

"No."

"Would you rather bet on the Queen of Hearts?"

Ossie was now determined to win back his money. He remembered cricket. When you lose a wicket you should not panic, for this may cause other wickets to fall. It was the time to keep your nerves, to be calm and to dig in. He picked up the card which he felt sure was the correct one.

But he was wrong again.

"When you buy inthuranth you take a chanth," said the gambler. "You juth might need it if you get thick, or a hurricane blow down your houthe. The Ace of diamonds!"

Bowling at the leg stump, Ossie picked a card, and lost again.

"Run boy!" said one of the men, "run with your money!"

Ossie was now down to the single coin with which he began. The urge to try and win back the money was very strong. But he could lose his bulla cake if he lost again.

"When playing football, if you don't shoot you don't score," said the gambler. "Shoot boy. Shoot. Ace of Diamonds!"

"No," said Ossie, "game done!"

There was a flash of anger on the gambler's face.

"What you mean 'done', boy? Play the game!"

"Ossie!" It was his father's voice, and Ossie turned and saw his father at the other end of the piazza. "Come here, Ossie. Your mother wants you."

"One more game, boy," demanded the gambler.

"Follow me," said his father as he began walking away.

"I want to buy a bulla cake," pleaded Ossie.

"Awright."

Ossie went into the shop.

"Serve!" he called out as he rattled the coin on the counter.

Maas Thom came through the door, his face calm and serene in the light of the Tilley lamp which hung from the ceiling.

"Please serve me one bulla cake, Maas Thom," said Ossie.

"Sure, young Johnny."

He opened the glass case, and lifted the cake with a tong, wrapped it in brown paper and handed it to Ossie.

"Thank you," said Ossie as he placed the coin on the counter. Maas Thom picked it up and placed it in the till.

Ossie bit into the brown, moist cake which was flavoured with ginger. He chewed and swallowed hungrily. It was less than the bully beef and bread he had dreamt about, but he was grateful for it. At least he was paying for it with his own hard-earned pocket money, he told himself.

"Gone, Maas Thom," he said.

"Bye son."

He stepped out onto the piazza.

"Come back mi fren!" called the gambler who was now alone at the table, with the tall man standing behind him.

Ossie joined his father, and they began walking side by side down the road.

"You lost any money?" asked his father.

"No."

"Stay away from that samfie man. He isn't even a real gambler, for the whole thing is fixed. The tall man is his confederate. I don't gamble. If you get addicted to that thing, dog nyam your supper."

"Yes, Papa."

They entered the house.

"Ossie, would you like some bread and cheese?" his mother called from her bedroom.

"Yes mama," he replied.

THE
JOB

One morning Ossie was running his wheel to school. The wheel was a bicycle rim with the spokes removed. He propelled it by keeping a stick in the groove and pushing it forward. The wheel banged noisily on the asphalt which had been recently laid before an election. The morning was fresh and beautiful, and Ossie was enjoying the feel of the wind on his face.

As he approached Mama D's house he saw her standing at the gate. She was wearing her usual white head-tie and apron. A widow, she was renowned for her cooking skills, and for running a boarding house much favoured by teachers. She was a friend of his parents.

"Morning Ossie. I have been waiting for you. Please ask your mother for permission to do a job for me on Saturday. I would like you to weed my garden."

"Yes mam," said Ossie as he resumed running his wheel.

With permission granted, Ossie set off for Mama D's home after breakfast the following Saturday. He carried his father's hoe on his left shoulder, and his father's cutlass in his right hand. He had observed his father weeding his fields, and he was accustomed to weeding his mother's garden, so he felt comfortable about his ability to do the job. He whistled as he walked, not as skillfully as Mr. Llewellyn, but he tried his best.

He walked up the gradient to Mama D's house. It was a large wooden building, one of the largest in the district, with a zinc roof and a verandah with rails which overlooked the main road. With breakfast over, Mama D was in the outside kitchen washing dishes. Ossie went to the door and greeted her.

"Morning Mama D."

"Morning Ossie. You come early. You are a man with a sense of time. You know where the garden is so go right ahead. I will call you for a snack later, and then for lunch."

"All right mam."

The garden was behind the kitchen, and afforded a magnificent view of the mountains and valleys. Ossie paused for a few moments to take it in. The sun was ascending the sky, and Ossie knew he would work all day under its steady and relentless stare. The house was on the eastern side of a hill, and the shadow cast by the sinking sun would give him some relief in the afternoon. But right now he felt very fresh and enthusiastic, so he began working among the roses, zinnias and chrysanthemums.

Everyone knew that this garden, with its white fence, was Mama D's pride and joy. Especially since the passing of her husband, cultivating it became her therapy. It helped her deal with the loss of the man who owned considerable property, including the shop that Maas Thom rented, and several acres of land. Her husband had been a good manager of things. Now she focused on her church, her boarding house and her garden. Ossie felt he was working in a special and sacred place.

"You are doing well, Ossie," said Mama D when she came to look at his work at mid-morning. "Come and have a cool drink."

He followed her to the kitchen and she handed him a glass of limeade, followed by a saucer with slices of bun and cheese. This was just what he needed. As he ate he heard piano music coming from the house. He recognized the Jamaican folksongs, "Shine Eye Gal" and "Gimme Back Me Shilling".

"Sounds like one of the teachers playing," observed Ossie.

"Miss Jackson. She is a fine pianist."

"I wonder what is that piece she is playing now? I have never heard it before, but I like it."

"Go ask her."

Ossie thanked Mama D for the refreshment. Then he climbed the steps and went into the house, with the music getting louder as he approached. He crossed the floor of the dining room and stood at the open door of the drawing room. Miss Jackson was sitting at the piano and was very absorbed in her playing. She had chocolate coloured skin, a beautiful profile, and her hair hung to her shoulders. She was wearing a green dress. Ossie stood silently and listened until she finished the piece.

"Good morning, Miss Jackson."

"Oh!" she said as she turned to him, a look of surprise in her dark-brown eyes.

"I am Ossie. I am weeding Mama D's garden."

"Oh yes. She told us about you. How is it going?"

"Very well. What is the name of that piece you just played?"

"Beethoven's 'Moonlight Sonata'."

"I like it. Who is Beethoven?"

"A great German composer. He composed some of his greatest music while he was deaf."

"How is that possible, mam?"

"I suppose he could hear the music in his imagination."

Ossie heard a sound on his right, and a Chinese young woman with long, black hair and almond eyes emerged from the bedroom. She was wearing a white blouse and tight red pants. She had a book in her right hand.

"Miss Chin See, this is Ossie. He is weeding the garden."

"Hello Ossie," she said with a smile." You are from here, so you may be able to answer my question." She beckoned to him with her finger to follow her to the verandah. Once there she pointed to the mango tree between the house and the road. "Why does that tree bear two different species of mangoes? I am a town girl and don't know much about trees."

44

Ossie was glad that he knew the answer. "It isn't one tree. There are two trees, but they grew so close the trunks merged and they look like one."

"Really! Well you have solved the mystery. For it seemed like a botanical impossibility to me."

"I have to go back to work now."

"Sure. After your work I would to ask you to do something for me."

"Yes, mam."

Ossie stopped at the kitchen to ask Mama D's permission to do some budding and grafting. He explained that Mr. Llewellyn had taught the boys how to do these things during their gardening class. Mama D agreed.

Ossie worked to the accompaniment of Miss Jackson's piano music. When he recognized pieces he whistled along with them. The two teachers were so beautiful he couldn't decide which one he admired most. He noticed the scent of the roses as he worked.

Near noon, after Miss Jackson and Miss Chin-See had eaten, Mama D called Ossie to lunch in the dining room. He was looking forward to tasting her hand. She did not disappoint him. He sat down to a meal of green gungo peas and saltfish cooked in coconut rundown, with escallion and tomatoes, and accompanied with slices of boiled yellow yam and green bananas. Then he washed it down with a glass of soursop juice. The food was so good he felt he could work for three days straight. Refreshed and rejuvenated, he returned to work.

The sun had been behind the hill for a couple of hours when Ossie began his final task, the building of a compost heap. Then he went to the end of the garden and surveyed his handiwork. He felt satisfied. He went to the kitchen to report to Mama D. She accompanied him back to the garden, and studied it for a few moments.

"Very good, Ossie. The garden looks brand new."

"Miss Chin See asked me to do something for her."

"Go right ahead."

Ossie found Miss Chin See sitting in a large wooden chair on the verandah. She was reading the book he had noticed earlier, and now he could make out its title and author: Banana Bottom by Claude McKay. He recognized the author's name, for Mr. Llewellyn had taught his class two poems by him, "Flame Heart" and "The Spanish Needle". The teacher hadn't said so, but Ossie had inferred that the poet was Jamaican, since he wrote about things that he recognized.

"Ossie, do you know Mr. Rainsford?"

"Yes, mam."

"Please take this to him for me." She handed him a sealed envelope with Mr. Rainsford's name on it. "Money is in it, so be careful. He will give you something for me."

"Yes, mam."

Ossie walked across the square and turned right onto the parochial road. He went uphill for about a quarter of a mile, and soon arrived at Mr. Rainsford's gate. The name of the house, "Relentless" was written in Old English on a strip of wood and nailed to a cedar tree. It was the only house in Clifton that had a name, and Ossie believed that Mr. Rainsford had learnt this in England. He also spoke a bit like the BBC news on the radio. There was also a sign which said, "Beware of Bad Dog".

"Hold dog!" Ossie called out loudly, and the dog responded by barking vociferously. "Hold dog!" he called out again.

"Come in," said a woman's voice. "The dog is chained."

Ossie opened the squeaky wooden gate and went in. The big black dog lunged fiercely at him, but was restrained by its chain. It kept up its barking. Miss Edna, Mr. Rainsford's wife, was sitting on a bench in a corner and washing clothes in a wooden tub. Ossie greeted her and told her his mission.

"Ranny! Somebody come to you!" she called out in a very powerful voice.

A few moments later, Mr. Rainsford came out to the verandah. He was tall, coal-black, and wore a felt hat, blue shirt and flannel pants.

"What can I do for you young man?" he said as he examined Ossie carefully.

"Miss Chin See sent this," said Ossie as he handed him the envelope. Mr. Rainsford tore it open and examined its contents.

"You are Maas Johnny's little boy, aren't you?"

"Yes sah. I am Ossie. I just finished weeding Mama D's garden."

"I see."

Mr. Rainsford crossed the yard and went into the outside kitchen. He came out with a basket of vegetables, some of which Ossie had never seen before. He handed the basket to Ossie.

"These are Chinese vegetables," he said when he noticed that Ossie had been studying them closely. "Pak Choy, Chinese broccoli, Chinese cabbage. Miss Chin See asked me to plant them for her."

"I didn't know that Chinese vegetables are different from other vegetables," said Ossie.

"Some of them are. Tell Miss Chin See thanks for me."

"Yes sah. Gone Maas Rainsford. Gone Miss Edna."

"Bye Ossie," said Mr. Rainsford.

"Walk good," said Miss Edna.

When he returned to Mama D's home, the two teachers were sitting on the verandah. Miss Chin See was still absorbed in Claude McKay's book, and Miss Jackson was reading a newspaper. Ossie mounted the steps and handed the basket to Miss Chin See. He conveyed Mr. Rainford's thanks.

"Thank you, Ossie," she said as she looked at the vegetables with smiling anticipation. "We will be having Chinese food for dinner tomorrow. I am teaching Mama D how to cook it. Use this to buy a pencil or an exercise book." She handed Ossie some money. He was reluctant to accept it but he did not want to hurt her feelings.

"Thanks, mam," he said.

Then he went to the kitchen to say goodbye to Mama D.

"You been a real man-a-yard here today, Ossie," she said. Ossie smiled but said nothing. "This is for your labour," she said as she handed him an envelope. Then she gave him a white plastic bag. "The cake is for your parents. But the lump of icing sugar is for you alone."

"Thanks, mam!" said Ossie as he looked at the contents of the bag with great anticipation.

"You worked well today, Ossie. Thank you very much."

"My pleasure mam. Gone Mama D."

"Bye son."

He then said goodbye to the two teachers.

"Goodbye, Ossie. Work hard at your books," said Miss Chin See.

"One day I will play some more music for you, Ossie," said Miss Jackson.

Ossie went down the gradient, with his father's hoe on his left shoulder, and the cutlass in his right hand.

"Ossie earned some pocket money today," his mother told his father during supper.

"What you going to do with it?" asked his father.

"Buy a book," replied Ossie.

"A book! I thought you would buy a shirt or some socks," said his father.

"No, I want a book. When I grow up I want to be a teacher like Mr. Llewellyn. And to be a teacher you have to read plenty books."

"So which book you going to buy?" asked his mother.

"Banana Bottom by Claude McKay."

"Do whatever you want," said his mother.

His mother served slices of Mama D's cake for dessert. It was moist and delicious. Ossie said he would save the icing sugar for the following day.

He intended to use part of the money to buy Christmas presents for his parents. Perhaps he would get a bottle of perfume for his mother and a cake of sweet soap for his father. But he wanted to keep all this as a surprise. So he ate his cake with relish, but silently. He was happy with his day.

THE
FRIEZE

Maas Johnny's cow had a calf and began giving rich, creamy milk which was in great demand in the community. It became one of Ossie's morning chores to take bottles of milk to customers in the district. His father began milking the cow while it was still dark, and, one morning, as daylight was becoming visible, Ossie set off for Mr. Andy "Asunu" Powell's home. Children like Ossie had to address the retired jockey as 'Maas Andy', but everybody else, including his thousands of fans across the island, simply called him 'Asunu'. It was an ironic name, for 'Asunu' meant elephant, the name of a character in Anancy stories, but Maas Andy was a very small man. After a distinguished career, he was thrown by a horse and was badly injured. He was now an invalid.

Ossie left the house, and as he arrived at his gate he was surprised to see Maas Andy's big white horse, Mountain Mist, trotting down the road towards him. Steve, Maas Andy's stocky eighteen year-old son, held the rope which was attached to the horse's bridle, and was moving alongside the animal as he tried to control the huge and powerful beast. This was the biggest and most dangerous looking animal Ossie had ever been so close to, and when he looked into the creature's blazing eyes he felt a great terror. He climbed up on the bank to get out of the way.

Steve burst out laughing. "She nah trouble you, man," he said. "I am giving her some exercise. She has a race coming up."

"Race?" asked Ossie.

"Yes. A man named Roy Martin from down Petersville challenge us to a race. We never refuse a challenge."

"When?"

"Next week Friday, up at the race course."

Steve and the horse had now passed Ossie and were turning the bend. Ossie came down from the bank and began walking along the road. He knew that the plateau between Clifton and his school was called Race Course, but he had never seen any races there. But he had heard his father say that in olden days, when there used to be a monthly animal market in the square, they used to race horses and donkeys there. Ossie was becoming interested in this race. Perhaps he and his schoolmates would be able to watch it from the hillside behind the playfield which overlooked the race track.

He found Maas Andy sitting on his verandah and sipping his usual coffee from a white enamel mug. Maas Andy wore a white t-shirt and grey pants. His walking stick was leaning against the wall beside him.

"Morning Maas Andy."

"Morning, Ossie. Miss P is in the kitchen."

Ossie stood at the door of the kitchen and watched as Miss P blew at the coals, trying to get the fire going. She was a stout woman, and wore a white head-tie and a loose frock. Ossie waited until the flames sprang up.

"Morning, Miss P."

"Morning, Ossie," she said as she turned to him. She came to the door and took the bottle. Her eyes were red from the smoke. "This milk is so good. How is Miss Ona and Maas Johnny?"

"Fine, mam. Gone, mam."

"Bye, Ossie."

Ossie paused in front of the verandah, for he felt like having a little chat with Maas Andy. He felt it was probably a very lonely life staying at home most of the time. Maas Andy's daughter was away at college. Steve took care of the horse, and was also learning carpentry.

"You used to ride Mountain Mist, Maas Andy?" asked Ossie.

"Yes, son. She is the best horse I ever rode." His voice was hoarse and he cleared his throat. "I won many trophies with her, and I have them on a shelf in the living room. I was Champion Jockey one year, thanks to her." There was a look of sadness in his eyes as he continued. "Both of us came to an end at the same time. With her days over, they wanted to put her to sleep, and to turn her into dog food and glue. But I begged for her. So they gave her to me as my retirement present. Both of us spending our retirement years together."

"Steve told me about the race coming up."

Maas Andy chuckled. "There will be betting, so some people will win some money. I hope I will be one of them. But it will be a fun thing too. Steve will ride her. He would make a good jockey, but he says he wants to do carpentry. I won't even be able to see the race. But I think the old girl going to show them that she still has some fire in her."

"I have to get ready to go to school, so gone Maas Andy."

"Bye, son."

The following morning Ossie approached the house via the path to the northern tank that supplied the district. He passed the people who were getting water, and then went up the hill. At the top of the spur he paused to watch Mountain Mist cavorting in the paddock. She was running around and kicking her hind legs in the air. It seemed she was longing for a good race. Then she paused to look at Ossie, and to his surprise she began walking towards him. He took control of his fear. She came up close and he patted her forehead and stroked her face. She whinnied, a very happy sound, he thought. Then she moved away and resumed running around the paddock.

The next morning Ossie took a mango for her. He did not know if horses ate mangoes, but he was eager to find out. But what if she

51

swallowed the seed and it choked her? So when she came up to him he cut a slice of the fruit and offered it to her. She ate it eagerly, and he fed her the rest. In fact, it seemed she loved beefy mangoes as much as he did.

A few mornings later, Steve was with her as he passed.

"Oi Ossie! You want a ride?" he called out, with a big grin on his round face.

"Me?"

"Yes, you. Deliver the milk and come back."

Ossie had never ridden an animal, and the thought excited him. Within minutes he was at the paddock. Steve opened the gate and let him in and then closed it again. Mountain Mist was wearing a yellow pad on her back. Steve began adjusting the stirrups to fit the length of Ossie's legs. Then he helped Ossie to mount the horse. The feel of the animal under him was so different from that of the seats of trucks, cars and buses. With the gate of the paddock locked, he knew that Mountain Mist could not gallop away with him. Steve put the leather strap in his hand. The horse moved forward and began circling the paddock. It was great fun and Ossie began laughing. The horse stopped, and before Ossie saw that she had bent her neck down to crop some grass, he found himself lying on his back in front of her. Steve was laughing hard.

"One more time Ossie!" he called out. "One more time. Get back on her!"

He helped Ossie back on the horse. This time Ossie kept his eyes on her head and neck as she walked. In a few minutes he got the hang of it and he was guiding her around the paddock. He found himself anticipating her movements. A bond of communication was developing between them.

"You going turn a jockey, Ossie," said Steve laughing.

"I don't think so, but you never can tell."

With the ride over Ossie thanked Steve for the experience. Then they talked about the upcoming race. Steve then told Ossie about what was involved in taking care of a horse. It was a lot of hard work, he said, but he enjoyed riding her.

"You can fall off a house, as well as off a horse," he said. "But I prefer to make something that can stand up in the wind and rain, than to gallop around a track. My father loved it, but it is not for me."

"I don't want to be late for school," said Ossie. "See you later."

On the afternoon of the big race, Ossie and some of his schoolmates sat on the grass patch under a bamboo chump which overlooked the race track. In the distance at the start, they could see the two horses with their riders moving about. They would be able to see the start and the first few furlongs of the race, after which the horses would disappear behind the trees which hid the bend in the track. The horses would emerge from the trees for the final stretch, and they would be able to see them as they approached the winning post. A crowd was assembled to watch the finish, and vendors could be seen selling ice cream, fudges, coconut cakes, peanuts, puddings and other snacks of that kind.

"I am betting on Brown Girl in the Ring," said Phonso, naming Roy Martin's chestnut.

"I would never bet on any horse," said Brightly. "You ever hear of a horse betting on people?"

"The horses would lose plenty money," said Washie.

"Just like the big people," quipped one of the girls.

It was a long wait before the race started, for it seemed as if they were having disagreements at the starting line. The horses kept turning, and moving backwards and forwards. They finally got them lined up, with their backs turned in the direction of the winning post. The starter dropped the flag, the jockeys spun their horses around and they were off.

The children sprang to their feet as the two horses sped, neck to neck, along the opening stretch. Ossie thought that Steve looked very professional as he stood in the stirrups with his head and trunk bent forwards as he urged his horse on. Mountain Mist was a streak of white, and Brown Girl in the Ring, sleek and muscular, was matching strides with her. They disappeared behind the trees.

"Come on, Mountain Mist!" yelled Ossie. "Mountain Mist! Mountain Mist!"

All eyes were focused on the edge of the trees where the head of the leading horse would be the first to appear. They knew that behind the trees the horses would have to climb a gradient, and that this would be a test for them. It seemed as if the horses were behind the trees for ages, but a great shout went up from the children when Mountain Mist appeared, and sprinted in a flash towards the winning post, with Brown Girl in the Ring now in futile pursuit. The spectators could be seen shouting, laughing and shaking each other's hands.

"What did you expect?" said Phonso. "Mountain Mist is an experienced racehorse."

"But she is getting old," said Ossie, "and Brown Girl is much younger."

"Old broom knows the corner," said the girl who had spoken earlier.

Ossie was delighted with the victory. He was pleased for Mountain Mist, for Steve, and most of all for Maas Andy who had no doubt won some much needed money. The children began to disperse, and Ossie wended his way home.

The following afternoon, after his chores of collecting firewood and fetching water from the tank, Ossie sat on the verandah with his exercise book contemplating his homework: an essay entitled "A Duppy Story". He was awakened from his reverie by the sound of footsteps coming down the path. He looked up and saw his Uncle Basil approaching, coming to pay a visit during his brief vacation. He was a slender, sepia-coloured man with thoughtful eyes, and he was already balding on the top of his head. Ossie noticed that he was carrying a folded newspaper in his hand.

"Sir Oswald Johnson!" he greeted Ossie cheerfully as he entered the yard.

"Good afternoon, Uncle Basil," said Ossie.

"I brought you a Gleaner," he said as he handed the paper to Ossie.

"Thank you, Sir," said Ossie as he took the famous newspaper.

"Where is your mother?"

"In the kitchen."

Ossie heard him calling out "Ona! Ona!" as he went in search of his sister.

Ossie opened the paper eagerly. He seldom had the opportunity to read newspapers. From time to time Mr. Llewellyn loaned his copies to the class, but apart from the teachers, few people in the district read newspapers. As Ossie read he noticed that the stories were mostly about politics and crime. But he enjoyed the sports section which had a photograph of a famous horse winning a race, as well as stories and photographs of cricketers, boxers and athletes whose names he had heard on the radio. He loved the comic strips, especially "Blondie", "The Phantom" and "Peanuts". It was while viewing the comic strips and admiring their artistry that he got an idea. Instead of writing a duppy story, he would draw a comic strip of one. He would base it on his dream of the previous night.

In the dream he was leaving home and arrived at the gate. He saw a riderless motorcycle coming down the road towards him. The motorcycle moved towards him and he tried to get out if its way but it kept following him. He began running down the road with the motorcycle chasing him. He turned to look and saw that it was transformed into Mountain Mist. He slowed down, but when he turned to look again Mountain Mist was now transformed into a fierce rolling calf with fiery eyes, with its chain dragging on the ground. Terrified, Ossie climbed into a mango tree. The rolling calf kept running around the tree and mooing up at him. It kept doing this for a long time, and it was clear it had no intention of going away. Then Ossie got an idea. He broke off a branch of the tree and began feeding the rolling calf with the leaves. The beast ate hungrily and wanted more and more. When it was satisfied, it lay down at the foot of the tree and began chewing its cud. Ossie got another idea. He jumped from the tree, right onto the animal's back, and he grabbed its horns. The rolling calf sprang to its feet and began running up the road. Ossie held on as firmly as he could. Then it turned into Mountain Mist. As the horse was galloping under the beefy mango tree, Ossie reached up and grabbed a branch. Mountain Mist galloped away from under him and he was left hanging safely from the branch. He woke up sweating, but relieved to be safe.

On a rough piece of paper, he broke the story down into frames.

Then he began drawing. In the background he could hear Uncle Basil and his mother speaking in the kitchen. A few minutes later Uncle Basil walked past the verandah and told him goodbye. He thanked him for the paper again, and resumed his drawing.

The class was busy writing in-class essays while Mr. Llewellyn sat at his desk marking scripts.

"Come here, Oswald Johnson," said the teacher.

Ossie went up to the desk.

"So you drew your essay instead of writing it. Why?" He gave Ossie a penetrating stare.

"I just felt like it Sir, I saw some comics in the Gleaner."

"I recognize the motorcycle and the rolling calf. But what about the horse?"

"It is a real horse, Sir," he replied, but he refused to respond to the teacher's questioning eyes asking for more. He did not want to speak about Mountain Mist. He would let the drawings speak for themselves.

"This is very unorthodox, but I will allow it," said the teacher. "You have a talent, boy. And a good imagination. You could become a cartoonist one day. I gave it an A."

"Thank you, Sir!" said Ossie, smiling. It was his third A that term. The first had been for science and the second for English, but this was the sweetest of them all, he thought.

"In fact, I want you to turn it into a frieze," the teacher continued.

"A what, Sir?"

'A frieze is a band of pictures that tell a story. I will give you cartridge paper, paint and brushes. Work on it during handicrafts."

"Thank you, Sir."

Ossie became absorbed in his frieze and worked with great enthusiasm. His classmates watched with fascination as the pictures formed under his fingers. When it was finished Mr. Llewellyn mounted it on the wall of the classroom, and invited students and teachers to look at it. Ossie was amazed at the variety of responses, both the praise and the criticism, but for the most part the responses were favourable.

"The boy is a born artist," said the headmaster. "He could become another Albert Huie."

"We knew that there is something in him," said Miss Chin See, and Miss Jackson nodded in agreement.

"What a way the rolling calf resemble Phonso!" said Washie with a laugh.

"I love the white horse," said Paulette. "She resembles Mountain Mist. See your drawings in the Gleaner one day, Ossie."

Ossie wrote to Uncle Basil, who was now in England, and told him the story of the newspaper and the frieze. A few months later a packet arrived from him. It had such fascinating stamps Ossie decided he would take up stamp collecting as a hobby. He opened the packet eagerly. It contained several comic books. In the accompanying letter Uncle Basil congratulated him on his artistic success, and urged him to study the comics, for one day the country might develop an animation industry, and there could be a place for him in it. Ossie's mother looked at the comic books with some suspicion, but she seemed pleased that one of them was an adaptation of William Shakespeare's Julius Caesar.

"Study them," she said, "and write to Uncle Basil at once."

THE
MAGICIAN

When the bell rang for the morning recess, the children poured out of the school into the yard with exultant cries of freedom. Ossie was among them. He began heading for the vendor who sat under the jackfruit tree with her glass-case of snacks on her lap. He was in the mood for a big, juicy coconut cake. But he was distracted by the sight of children gathered in front of a man on the other side of the yard, so he stopped to look. It was Popsi who used to work as a sideman on Mr. Stuart's truck, and he was putting on some kind of performance. Ossie decided to postpone the coconut cake and he joined the crowd to watch.

Popsi asked a girl to come forward, and one of them, giggling self-consciously, went up to him. He announced that he would make her lay an egg. He showed them his empty palms, and then he held his right hand under the hem of the girl's dress, said "Boom Shaka Shaka!" and lo and behold, a white egg appeared in his palm. There were bursts of applause and laughter from the children.

Then, Popsi raised his right hand and plucked a white dove out of the air. The children gasped in amazement. Ossie moved forward so he could take a closer look at these wonders.

"I want a hat," said Popsi.

The only boy in the crowd who was wearing a cap stepped forward and offered it to Popsi. "Boom Shaka Shaka!" said Popsi as he pulled a brown-and-white guinea-pig from it. There was applause and exclamations of amazement. By now Ossie had forgotten about the coconut cake. He watched with delight and admiration as Popsi continued to dazzle them with his extraordinary deeds. Then the bell rang and jolted Ossie back to reality. The recess was over and it was now time for arithmetic.

But Ossie found it difficult to concentrate on the problems he was asked to solve. Popsi's magical world seemed a lot more fascinating. There he could see the impossible realized. It seemed the opposite of the iron rules of numbers.

That evening on his way home from school he saw Popsi standing on a bank beside the road, and staring reflectively down into the bushes.

"Good evening Mr. Magician," said Ossie.

Popsi turned to him. "Oh! So you were at school today."

"Where you learn to do those things?" asked Ossie.

"Boy, is a long story," said Popsi as he scratched his chin.

"I did poorly at school. I am dyslexic, but didn't know it at the time. Had difficulty reading and spelling. A brain condition. But people said I was a dunce." He noticed that Ossie was listening carefully, so he continued. "One year Teacher went to England on a bursary, and they sent an old man, a retiree, to act for him. This man was a beater, and he kept a stack of canes beside his desk. One day he called me up to the front of the class for a beating. I wasn't even sure what I had done. But I decided that there was no way he was going to beat me. So I grabbed my books and sprinted through the door. Never went back to that school. Until today. Wanted to show them that I can do things too."

"Your parents didn't send you back?"

"Granny Sue, who raised me, wanted me to go back. Said I should try and take the education. But my mind was made up. So I got a job as a sideman on a truck. That took me to Kingston nearly every day and I fell in love with the city. I quit the sideman's job and became a

59

handcart man. I lived with relatives in a tenement yard in Rema. That was where I met Rashford "Houdini" Wellington the great magician. He was my neighbor. You ever heard about him?"

"No."

"He stowed away on a ship to Sweden. They put him in prison, but they taught him to read and write. In the prison library he found a book on magic and taught himself. After he was deported to Jamaica he made money performing magic on the streets. An impresario saw him and invited him to perform on stage at the Carib theatre. He gave it to them! His picture was in the newspaper and he got a job performing at a hotel on the north coast. He was off and running I tell you. Rashie taught me really everything I know."

"And what are you doing now?"

"I came up for Granny Sue's funeral. Spending some time with my people. Eat some country food. Breathe some fresh air. Then go back to town and try to get a better job."

"The magic should help you," said Ossie. "If you can do all these amazing things, finding a job should be as easy as cheese."

Popsi burst out laughing. "No man! Magic is just tricks."

"So you not an obeah-man?"

Popsi was laughing even louder now. "I don't have anything to do with obeah and witchcraft."

"Can you heal people? Like Brother Paul?"

"No, man. I can only make them laugh and perhaps feel a little better."

"So you don't work miracles? Like Jesus?"

"You taking me into deep waters there boy. But I am no Brother Paul. Anybody can learn magic. Even you."

"Really?"

"You learn certain skills with your hands and fingers. But most of all you learn how to make people's brains do the work for you."

"Teach me, then."

"Sure."

So Ossie became Popsi's apprentice. Many evenings after school Popsi waited for him at that very spot on the road, and taught him tricks, beginning with the very simple ones. Then Ossie began visiting him at Granny Sue's former home on the other side of the river. There, Popsi introduced him to some of the objects and devices of the trade.

Ossie also remembered the story of Rashford "Houdini" Wellington's learning experience in the library in Sweden. So during the lunch hour one day he examined the bookcase beside the headmaster's desk, and sure enough there was a book on magic in it. He asked the teacher to lend it to him.

"What you want to do with magic, boy?" he demanded. "There is no magic in life except hard work, honesty and sacrifice."

"There is science and arithmetic in it Sir."

"Really!" he exclaimed as he examined Ossie for signs of some prankish excuse.

"Yes Sir. I could show you."

"All right then."

Ossie found much of Mr. Llewelyn's science and arithmetic in the book. He became absorbed in his new pursuit. He concluded that magicians used the laws of reality to create the appearance of unreality. He recalled that Popsi had once said that a magician is a kind of artist who uses science, and he was beginning to see why. When the headmaster announced an upcoming school concert, and invited pupils to inform their class teachers about items they would like to perform, Ossie saw his chance. He told Mr. Llewellyn he would like to perform some magic.

"Magic, Oswald?"

"Yes Sir."

"What do you know about magic?"

"I have been studying it, sir."

The class tittered.

"Ossie working with duppy," said Phonso with a laugh.

"Duppy nothing!" said Ossie with some heat. "It is all about tricks, Sir."

"All right, then."

Ossie asked his mother to make a red cape for him to wear during his performance.

"Boy, I don't like this foolishness you know," she said.

"Mama, there is science in it," he protested.

"Sc-iance. Sc-iance. We didn't send you to school to become any sc-iance-man!"

"This is real science, Mama. The kind we study at school. This is not any sc-iance or obeah."

She relented and made the cape.

On the day of the concert, after school, Ossie joined the other boys in preparing the schoolroom for the event. They pushed the blackboard-partitions and desks to the side of the building, and arranged the seats in rows. They positioned the platform which would be the stage at the northern end. A table and chair were placed at the northwestern corner for the master of ceremonies. Under the supervision of Mr. Llewellyn and two other male teachers, they erected a thatched dressing room outside, behind the stage area. With the building ready, Ossie hurried home to have his dinner and to get ready for the concert.

He and his parents set off at around 7:00 p.m. It was an-hour's walk uphill to the school. His mother wore a floral dress and a white hat. It was one of the rare occasions when Ossie saw his father wearing a suit. Ossie carried the tools of his trade and his cape in a suitcase.

Popsi, dressed in a red shirt and grey trousers, came to the dressing room to give Ossie some last minute tips about the tricks they had rehearsed together. "Sock it to them, boy," he said. "Make their jaws drop in amazement. Show them that magic is a fantasy of the mind!" They could hear the programme proceeding inside. Ossie waited nervously as he listened to the seemingly interminable songs, poems and skits, to the jokes of the chairman, at the applause of the audience. But what if his tricks didn't work? What if the audience didn't applaud? He tortured himself with his doubts. Finally, he heard the chairman say:

"And now we will have some magic by Oswald Johnson!" With his heart pounding he headed for the door.

He heard chuckles as he mounted the stage dressed in his red cape. But there was dead silence as he arranged his equipment. He could hear the gasps of horror as he swallowed a thread of razor blades, washed it down with a glass of water and then pulled it from his throat without any blood. The audience applauded. Then he passed a mango through a pane of glass. The applause was even louder now. He could hear the gasps of incredibility as he made a bank note keep changing its value before their eyes. He could now feel the audience with him as he continued to make the world a wonderful and extraordinary place where everything seemed possible. At the end of his act the applause was thunderous. Men put their fingers in their mouths and whistled.

"I would like to thank my teachers," said Ossie. "A special thanks to Mr. Agrippa "Popsi" Henry who taught me some of these tricks. I would like to ask him to stand and take a bow."

Popsi stood up and the audience turned to him and applauded. Ossie noticed people bending their heads to their neighbours to ask about Popsi. Words about his identity ran through the audience. Children who had seen him perform in the schoolyard told their parents about him. There was more applause as Ossie left the stage, triumphant.

"You were very good Ossie," said his mother while they were walking home. "But how did you get involved with Popsi?"

Ossie told them the story.

"Granny Sue had so much trouble with that boy," his mother continued. "Who would have thought he would become a magic-man?"

"He's very good," said Ossie.

"Boy, you better than Brer Anancy," said his father. "People going have to think twice before they trouble you!"

"They are just tricks, Papa."

The following day Ossie found himself the hero of his class.

"I have to ask Ossie to help me pass my exam," said Phonso.

"You going have to work hard, boy," replied Ossie.

"And you going have to think twice before you fight him," said Washie. "He might turn you into a green lizard!"

"Magic is an old practice," said Mr. Llewellyn sounding as if he had read up on the subject the night before. Then, starting with the story in Exodus 7: 10-12, of how the rods of Moses and Aaron became serpents and ate those of Pharaoh's magicians, he told them about magic through the ages.

"It contributed to the development of science," he continued. "Real science, not the sc-iance that our local people mean when they refer to obeah and the occult. But their use of the word is accurate in linking an earlier connection between the two. If our great, great grandparents could come back and see aeroplanes and cars, they would call it sc-iance. But now magic is mostly a form of entertainment, and great magicians earn a lot of money. It is all about the play between appearance and reality. Now let us do some real science and see the magic in reality."

That evening Ossie found Popsi waiting for him at the usual spot on the bank.

"I am proud of you youth," said Popsi. "You teach them. Perhaps you even taught the teachers a thing or two."

"What you going to do when you go back to town?"

"Back to my handcart. But the magic helps to take my mind off the rough life of the streets. But one day I am hoping I will follow Rashie and get a job in a hotel on the north coast."

"Good luck."

"More time my friend."

THE STRANGER

It was Saturday, the day of the big morning work. Ossie's mother awoke even earlier than usual to prepare breakfast for the men who would come to help her husband Maas Johnny clear a patch of land to plant sweet potatoes. As hosts, it was the responsibility of Ossie's parents to provide the men with a hearty breakfast, and all the rum they wanted. Maas Johnny would in turn help them with their fields. Maas Johnny left for the field at daybreak. Now it was Ossie's duty to assist his mother in preparing the breakfast and in transporting it to the field. As a rule, his mother kept him out of the kitchen, except to do manly things like husking and breaking coconuts, and opening tight bottles and jars. Now he stood near the door of the kitchen and waited for her commands and requests.

He observed as she prepared the food. She added flakes of washed saltfish, chopped escallion, and black pepper to the batter, and whipped the mixture with a spoon. She dropped spoonfuls of the batter into the hot coconut oil in the frying pan, and there was a constant hissing as the fritters were fried. The aroma of the fritters combined delightfully with that of the loaves of fresh, hard-dough bread that she began slicing as soon as the fritters were done. Then she began making the beverages the men would choose from: coffee, chocolate, mint tea or limeade. There were several bottles of rum and sodas on the table.

The men greeted his mother as they passed the kitchen on their way to the field. Some greeted Ossie by name, and a few called him 'son', 'youth man' or 'young Johnny'. Then a man Ossie had never seen before appeared. He was in his twenties, younger than all the other men. He had copper-coloured skin and one of the fancy American hairstyles Ossie had seen in his barber's magazines. The khaki shirt and pants he wore were of the most expensive and refined brand of that fabric, and they fitted tightly on his muscular, athletic body. He was carrying a brand new machete in his left hand.

"Morning Miss Ona," he said smiling mysteriously.

"Morning mi love," she replied. "Is who dat? I don't recognize that voice." She came to the door to look at the stranger.

"Is me Larry. Maas Ishy's nephew."

"Maas Ishy's nephew? He is my church brother. But I don't think I know you."

"I live in town. But I used to spend holidays up here when I was a boy. I am spending some time here, and heard about the morning work. I come to give a hand."

"Welcome mi love. Just follow that path. It will take you right to where the men will be working."

"Later," said Larry as he began walking down the path.

It was around 8:00 a.m., and the sun was over the mountain when Ossie and his mother set off for the field. Ossie balanced a tray of food on his head. His mother carried a basket on hers, and had a covered pail in her right hand. They walked carefully down the steep hillside path.

They arrived at the bit of level land which was shaded by a paper-skin mango tree, where the breakfast would be served. They could hear the sounds of the machetes chopping grass, and the men yelling and whooping. After they put down their loads Ossie went to the brink of the level to look. The seven men were furiously engaged in a grass-cutting contest to see who could first clear his stretch of bush up to the level. They had already cleared about a hundred yards up from the river.

Larry was on the left of the band of workmen, and was already way ahead of the others, who were now chopping even more fiercely as they tried to catch up with him. There was a grin on Larry's face as he responded to the good natured taunts, challenges and boasting of his competitors. Miss Ona stood beside Ossie and signalled to the men that breakfast was ready. But they were determined to complete the contest first. Larry was bent on a dramatic victory. Not only did he get to the level first, but, chopping vigorously with his left hand, he curved to the right and cut a victory arc above them. Then he sat on the ground and enjoyed a good laugh.

With the contest over, the men began assembling at the level for breakfast. "You still a young boy," said one of the men to Larry. "Hard life don't reach you yet."

"Watch me and him next time," said another. "I am going to teach that town-man a lesson!" With their clothes now soaked with sweat, the men sat on the grass.

Miss Ona began handing them plates of food and mugs and glasses of beverages. Their good natured bantering continued. Ossie felt pleased that he had seen them playing a game with their work, for it had made them seem like big boys.

Larry sat in the middle of the ground in what was almost a Buddha pose, and his expensive khaki outfit was now drenched with sweat. He was dominating the conversation.

"This country could feed itself if we put our minds to it," he said.

"Look at your plate," said Maas Zeke, who was balding and had a long sorrowful face. "The saltfish and the flour for the bread and fritters all come from overseas. Only the coffee and the coconut milk come from here."

"And the sugar," said Sarge, a light-skinned man with twinkling eyes.

"And that come from slavery," said Larry.

"I forgot about that," said Maas Zeke. "But it don't stop the coffee from tasting nice. Miss Ona! Miss Ona! Some more coffee, please!"

"Sure Maas Zeke," said Miss Ona as she brought the coffee pot over and poured the beverage.

"And look who is talking about growing more food. This town-man!" spat Maas Zeke.

"It doesn't matter who says it," declared Larry with some heat. "The question is whether it is true!"

"It is true," said Sarge. "I would be just as happy with bammy, callaloo and crayfish from the river."

"But look at us," said Maas Zeke. "Except for this young fella we are all old men. So who going to feed the nation?"

"Ossie! Ossie!" called Miss Ona. "Come help me with this jar of guava jelly!"

Ossie left the conversation and went to help his mother.

With the meal over, Ossie and his mother returned home with lighter loads on their heads. His mother began washing the dishes. She told him to do some school work until it was time for him to take more bottles of rum and sodas to the men. He sat at the dining table with his sketch pad and began drawing a picture of Larry winning the grass-cutting contest.

As he was going downhill with the bottles in a small basket in his hand, he could hear the men singing as they worked. He recognized the song "Bartilby" for he had heard it a couple of times before. The men were now beyond the level, and as he approached they began singing "Bring Me Half a Hoe". The rum, water, sodas and glasses were kept in the shade of the tree, and the men went there to help themselves whenever they felt like a drink. One of them, a stocky, round-faced man called Bimmock, followed Ossie to the level. He poured white rum in a glass, added a little water, raised the glass to his lips, threw back his head and swallowed in three gulps. Then he made a face. "Study your books, boy," he said. "This life is not for you." He went up the hill to rejoin the work-gang.

That evening while Ossie was doing his schoolwork at the dining table, he overheard his parents discussing Larry in the kitchen.

"He wants me to rent him a piece of land to do some farming," said Maas Johnny.

"Maas Ishy is a good man. If he is really his nephew."

"I don't see any resemblance. But is so him say."

"Where would you rent him?"

"I am thinking of the point down by the river."

"Give him a chance then, nuh."

"I will work out the rent with him."

Ossie began seeing Larry often when he passed through their yard on his way to his farm. The finger of land jutted to the river, and was bounded by tributaries of the river on its northern and southern sides. The soil was soft and sandy, good for sweet potatoes, Ossie had heard his father say. Larry passed nearly every weekday, with his hoe and machete. He greeted Ossie each time he saw him, and began laughing and joking with him. When he discovered that Ossie liked playing cricket he began calling him 'Skipper', and eventually just 'Skip' for short.

One day Ossie's mother asked him to take lunch to Larry. He set off with the white carrier, a bottle of orange soda, and a bottle-opener in his pocket. He went downhill, crossed one of the tributaries of the big river, went uphill alongside a yam field, then enjoyed the shade of a cool walk through a bamboo grove, and then went downhill towards Larry's potato field. He got to the shade of the hairy mango tree, and stood for a few moments and watched Larry working. He was shirtless, and his copper-coloured skin and deep chest were shining with sweat. He was chopping the earth fiercely, digging the potato hills with an intensity Ossie had never seen in a worker before. It was as if he were working something out of his system, losing it with the sweat that flowed from his body. He was chopping the earth as if his life depended on it.

"Oi Maas Larry!" called Ossie.

"Oi, is you, Skip," he replied looking up.

"Mama send lunch for you."

"Bless her."

Larry put his hoe aside and dried himself with a striped towel. He came towards Ossie and sat at the root of the mango tree. Ossie handed him the carrier and he opened it eagerly. He tackled the salt mackerel and St. Vincent yam with gusto. Then he took the soda, but before Ossie could pull the opener from his pocket, Larry opened it with his belt buckle. He swallowed the drink long and thirstily, after which he belched with deep appreciation.

"This land is nice to dig," he said. "It is very soft. Your father promised me some potato slips."

"You dig plenty hills already," said Ossie.

"Hey Skip!" said Larry changing the subject. "Who was Jamaica's first cricket hero?"

"Don't know."

"George Headley, man. He was the first man to score two centuries in a test at Lords. Who are the three Ws?"

"Worrel, Walcott and Weekes."

"Good boy! I hoped to be another George Headley someday."

"Then why not?"

"Boy, water more than flour," replied Larry as a shadow fell over his face. He suddenly seemed very tired and drained. "Stick to your books, Skip. Stick to your books. The lunch was very nice. Thank Miss Ona for me."

It was mostly sport that Larry and Ossie talked about each time he paused at the house for a little chat. Next to cricket, boxing seemed to be his other main interest. He told Ossie about early Jamaican boxers like Kid Silver and Lefty Flynn. He praised Norman Manley for forming the Jamaica Boxing Board of Control. Ossie was intrigued to hear about Jack Johnson the first black world heavyweight champion, and his famous and controversial fight with Jess Willard in nearby Havana. Larry re-enacted the commentary of famous fights he had seen on film, sometimes even singing the national anthems. Then he would say, "Study your books, Skip", and head for his field.

Larry reaped a big potato crop and sold the produce to higglers. One day he brought some of the choice potatoes as a gift for Miss Ona. She roasted and fried some, and used the others to make porridge and a pudding.

Some months later, the Baptist church was having an evangelistic crusade with services every night. One night Ossie and his friends went to have a look. They peered through the spaces between the oval-shaped stained-glass windows. The church was packed with worshippers, mostly women, but there were a few men in the back rows. The Rev. Winston Burchell was conducting the service. He was fat and dark-skinned, and his powerful voice seemed to be coming with some difficulty out of his thick neck. His white collar gleamed in contrast with his skin and black gown. Using a call and response method, he was leading the congregation through hymns, choruses and readings, and they were responding with ecstatic "Amens!" and "Praise the Lords!" to the texts as well as to his exhortations and admonitions. Then he preached a powerful sermon in which he described the hell to which unrepentant sinners would go. His images were so graphic Ossie could visualize the flames and devils, and he could almost smell the sulphur. Then the minister announced the altar call, and opened it with stirring hymns like "Behold me Standing at the Door" and "Come Ye sinners Poor and Wretched". The hymn "There Were Ninety and Nine that Safely Lay" was the straw that broke the camel's back of Larry's conscience, for much to Ossie's surprise, he saw him walking towards the altar. He wore a white shirt and grey pants, and now had a more modest haircut he was getting from Prendy the barber. When he arrived at the altar he turned to give his testimony.

"I come from a poor family, but I won a scholarship to go to a good high school in Kingston. I was good at my studies, and even better at sports. I represented my school in cricket and football. I took up amateur boxing and dreamt of fighting at the Olympics.

"But bad company mash me up. I wanted to show the other boys that I was badder than the baddest of them. I started to drink and smoke. Then I was into ganja. After that we got a gun.

"The first time we broke a shop it was for the fun of it. But the money felt sweet. So there was another and another. Then we started worrying about getting caught. So we killed one of the witnesses so she couldn't talk.

"It was me who fired the gun. I will never forget how I took a human life. And she was a good woman too. Owner of a gas station. Used to do plenty charitable work in the prisons and inner cities. And she had young children."

Larry began to sob. He covered his face with his hands and his body shook. The congregation began singing "Pass Me Not O Gentle Saviour". Larry was weeping bitterly now.

Ossie was shocked. Images of his acquaintance with Larry flashed through his mind. But now he felt he understood something of what had brought him back to the countryside of his childhood, and what had made him dig the potato hills with so much vigour and sweat.

"Larry is a murderer!" said Phonso.

"I wonder what parson going to do?" asked Washie.

Larry's confession brought the service to an end. The minister announced that the services would continue the following night, and for the rest of the week. He pronounced the benediction. Then he began leading Larry by the hand towards his car which was parked at the entrance to the building. Maas Ishy, in his pin-striped suit, followed them. Ossie and his friends hurried to the front so they could see better.

Maas Rashie, the District Constable, was waiting for them at the door. "You are under arrest," he said as he put the handcuffs on Larry's wrists.

"Get in the car," said the minister. "Let us take him to the police station right away."

There was a look of resignation on Larry's face as they ushered him into the back seat. Maas Ishy joined Maas Rashie and Larry in the back seat. The preacher got behind the wheel and his wife sat beside him.

Larry avoided looking into the face of anyone. There was now a crowd standing around the car. As the preacher started the engine and turned on the headlights, the crowd parted to make way. Ossie watched the rear lights as the car drove towards the exit. The brake -light came on as it slowed down at the gate, then went off again. The car disappeared into the night.

"Come, Ossie," he heard his mother say. "It is time to go home."

He followed his mother as she walked towards the gate. He could hear her firm footsteps on the grass. It was a dark night with no moon. The sky stared down coldly with its thousands of eyes. They walked in silence along the dark country road.

THE LOAN

As she did most Thursday mornings, Miss Evelyn, the higgler arrived early at Ossie's home to collect produce for the market. Miss Ona, his mother, was prepared. She had a pile of yams, sweet potatoes, dasheens, soursops, limes and sticks of sugar cane waiting in a corner of the kitchen. After greeting Miss Ona and having a brief conversation with her, Miss Evelyn skillfully packed the items into her basket. She was a stout and taciturn woman with a complexion like golden apples. Ossie was about to leave for school and he and Miss Evelyn walked together towards the gate.

"Higglering not easy me boy," she said, embarking on one of her rare monologues. "You have to walk all over the district to collect the goods, then you have to pack them into the crocus bags at the roadside. And on Thursday night you sit on the hard seat as you drive in the truck to the market in Kingston. You sleep in the market for two nights, carefully watching everything because of de tief dem. You haffi sweet-talk the customers to make them buy from you, and so that they become your regular customers. Then come Saturday you buy all the things that people from the district ask you to buy for them. And you buy things to bring back to the district to sell. And you have to keep track of all that business in yuh head. It not easy me boy."

"Gone, mam," said Ossie when they got to the gate.

"Study yuh books yuh hear."

"Yes, mam."

The following Sunday morning, Ossie performed one of his most pleasant chores. He went to Miss Evelyn's home to collect the items she had bought for his family with the money from their produce. She handed him a bag, and the aroma of the large, fresh hard dough bread made his mouth water. He also enjoyed the delightful scents of the rosewater, thyme and escallion. She also handed him a bottle of port. Then she gave him an envelope with the money that was left over. Ossie thanked her and turned to leave.

"Ossie, look what Mama brought for me from Kingston!" shouted Kingsley, Miss Evelyn's son of about Ossie's own age, as he emerged, grinning, from behind the house. He was wearing a red T-shirt with a series of arcs at the collar.

"It is a nice shirt," said Ossie. "I wish I had one like that."

"Ask Mama to buy one for you."

"I don't have any money."

"Borrow it," suggested Kingsley.

Ossie left the yard still thinking about the T-shirt. Perhaps he would be able to buy one with the money he was saving for Christmas, if they were still in style then. But should he borrow money to buy one? He had never borrowed money in his life. And if he borrowed money how would he pay it back?

The following day at school he set his mind on another item that he desired. A buxom, brown-skinned girl named Cherry, who was in the class above his, brought a used book she was selling over to Mr. Llewellyn, his teacher, and asked him to advertise it to the class. The teacher held up the blue book with white stripes before the class, and said it was entitled Robinson Crusoe, and was written by a man named Daniel Defoe in the 18th century. It was the story of a man who was shipwrecked alone on a deserted island and had to fend for himself. "But it is more than that," Mr. Llewellyn continued. "It is one of the first novels ever written in the English language, and even then, it dealt with the relations between the light-skinned and the darker-skinned people of the world, an issue that is still with us." He glanced at the cover and continued. "It is also recommended for Grade 5, your age group. Frankly, I think it is a must-read for every person in the world, and it has always been especially popular with boys." Ossie decided that he wanted to read this novel. The idea of a man fending for himself, alone on a deserted island, fascinated him. He wanted to buy it. But where would he get the money? He had very little in his savings box. "Get a loan!" he heard Kingsley saying to him.

The opportunity for the loan came sooner than he expected. During the next recess he was playing marbles with his friends when Washie suddenly exclaimed, "I am rich!"

"You what?" demanded Phonso.

"Rich. My father sent me some money from America. Dollars boy!"

"So what you going to do with the money?" asked Brightly.

"Mama say I should open a bank account. But I feel like running a boat with you guys: hot hard dough bread with butter, sardines and sodas!"

"You have my permission for the boat," said Phonso.

"But you should also save some," suggested Brightly.

"And you can give me a loan," said Ossie.

"Loan!" exclaimed Washie. "But how you going to pay me back?"

"I am saving my pocket money," said Ossie. "And I can ask Miss Evelyn to sell things in the market. Sometimes Miss Princess gives me a little money for my drawings. She puts them on cushions and things like that. She is even encouraging me to send cartoons to The Gleaner."

"The Gleaner!" exclaimed Phonso. "You think they would pay some little country boy like you for his drawings?"

"They pay all those people who draw in it," said Washie.

"And I am sure the postman knows where to find The Gleaner Company," said Brightly.

"I will have to discuss your loan application with my mother," said Washie to Ossie.

"Sure," said Ossie.

Ossie began fretting about repaying the loan even before Washie made up his mind. What if he couldn't repay the money? Still it would be nice to own either the T-shirt or the book. He was still undecided which one he would go for.

The following Saturday evening his father brought home a small newspaper published by one of the political parties. As he entered the living room he handed the paper to Ossie. As Ossie began reading, he saw a photograph of the minister of finance being welcomed by his colleagues at the airport. The minister carried an attaché case and had a big smile on his face as one of his colleagues was shaking his hand warmly. The article said the party was congratulating him for having secured a loan from an international agency. As Ossie's father re-entered the living room on his way to the bedroom Ossie told him about the article.

"Not me!" he replied. "If I borrow a dollar from a man I cannot sleep in my bed at night until I have repaid him. All these politicians know is how to beg and borrow. They going to borrow us into bankruptcy one day. You mark my word!" He walked away.

During their class on current affairs the following week, Ossie told Mr. Llewellyn about the article and asked him for his opinion on borrowing. The teacher walked over to the headmaster's bookcase and pulled out a big volume. He returned to the class and after flipping through the pages, he found what he was looking for. He read aloud an extract from Charles Lamb's "The Two Races of Men". According to Lamb, mankind can be divided into only two races: the borrowers and the lenders. In his view the borrowers are clearly the superior race. They tended to be portly, open-minded and generous, and contemptuous of money (especially when the money belongs to others). The lenders, in contrast, were meager, suspicious and servile. Without saying another word, Mr. Llewellyn returned the book to the case and moved on to the next topic.

The following morning, while Ossie was on his way to the tank to fetch water, he saw Mr. Stuart, the owner of much land and several motor vehicles, coming up the path from his house on his way to his car. After telling him good-morning, Ossie went straight to the point:

"What do you think of borrowing money, Sir?" Still breathing heavily from climbing the hill, Mr. Stuart, with his grey pants hanging below his paunch, and his white shirt fresh as the morning, looked carefully at Ossie, more carefully and with more interest than Ossie had ever seen him show in him before, and said:

"My boy, if you want a man to wish you well, to go down on his knees every night and pray to God to give you good health and much prosperity, owe him some money. In order to make people think about you day and night, you must owe them money. You may have heard the sayings: 'Never a lender or borrower be', and 'Lend only what you can afford to lose'. But I say there is nothing that is wrong with borrowing in itself. The important thing is what you do with the money you borrow. If you spend it on things that will only give you temporary pleasure, or depreciate in value – a car is worth less the moment you drive it out of the dealer's – then it is a foolish thing. But if you spend it on things that will appreciate in value, like land, a house or a good education, then it could make you better off in the long run. So think wisely, my friend." He began walking towards his car.

"Thank you, sir," said Ossie.

That night Ossie tossed in bed as he tried to decide. He would look handsome in the T-shirt, but before long it would be a mere rag. His teacher said that reading books like novels would improve his vocabulary and English, teach him things about life and the world, and that this could help him to pass his exams, and later be an asset to his career. Which was better: to be handsomely clothed or to be educated? Should he risk sleepless nights and the fear of debt such as his father experienced? Should he be an open-minded and superior man like Lamb's borrowers? Or should he be a shrewd investor like Mr. Stuart? With these questions on his mind he fell asleep.

He dreamt he saw his Uncle Basil with his white friends in a pub in England. They held mugs of beer in their hands. Uncle Basil raised his mug to him and said, "Cheers!" Ossie awoke. Next to his mother, Uncle Basil was the person who encouraged him most in his educational pursuits. He interpreted the dream as a sign that he should choose education. So he would opt for Robinson Crusoe.

Washie made the best case he could for Ossie as a loan risk, and his mother relented and approved the lending of the money. He took the money to school – it was now changed into local currency – and gave it to Ossie. During the recess Ossie went in search of Cherry and found her playing hop-scotch with some other girls. He waited until the game was over, and then went up to her and asked if the book was still available. She said it was. They went to her class and she took the book out of her bag. Ossie handed her the money and took the book from her. He went over to his class rejoicing quietly.

The first thing he did was look at the illustrations. There was a big one showing Crusoe with a parrot on his shoulder. Another showed Crusoe climbing a tree, an activity at which he himself was quite skilled. There was one that showed Crusoe with a gun, but Ossie was afraid of guns, including the one that Mr. Stuart used to shoot hawks. The others included portrayals of Crusoe salvaging items from the wrecked ship; a herd of wild goats (Ossie was taking care of a domesticated goat); and Crusoe shoving a canoe into the sea. But there was one which showed Crusoe with his foot on the head of a man who was lying on the ground. This was probably the dark-skinned man that Mr. Llewellyn had mentioned. This picture disturbed Ossie deeply. He returned to the front pages, and noticed that it was illustrated by someone named F. Cockerton. Perhaps one day there would be a book with the words, "Illustrated by Oswald Johnson", he told himself. He began reading the book eagerly.

But the problem of repaying the money was now even more worrisome to him. Desperate, he decided to take Miss Princess' advice and send some cartoons to The Gleaner. What did he have to lose? Only the money for the paper, the envelope and the stamp. He got the address from Mr. Llewelyn's copy of the newspaper. Without discussing it with anyone –he did not want anyone to mock or laugh at him if he failed—he posted the letter. But he soon stopped thinking about it. His little letter would be probably one of hundreds to arrive at the paper, and it was unlikely anyone would even read it. He became absorbed in his studies, and with giving Miss Evelyn produce from their land to sell in the market. Little by little he hoped to save the money to repay the loan.

A few weeks later he went to the post office to ask for letters, and was startled when Miss Princess handed him an envelope with his name typed on it, and the words, The Daily Gleaner, written in Old English, at the top left. His heart sank. Perhaps they were returning his drawings with a rejection note. With his heart pounding he tore the envelope open. There was a dated clipping from the newspaper with one of his cartoons on it. It showed a bent old man with a stick talking with a small boy in short pants and wearing glasses and with a book under his arm. "Little boy," says the old man, "what is green like grass but is not grass, juk like macca but is not macca, white like milk but is not milk?"

"Soursop, sah," replies the little boy. Ossie chuckled at the riddle he had first heard from his father, and which he had transformed into a cartoon. Then Ossie turned to the large cheque with his name printed on it. (This letter was the first time he was seeing his name in print, and it was his very first cheque.) The amount of money made him gasp. It was enough to repay the loan, and there would be some left over he could build on to buy the T-shirt. He yelled with joy! Miss Princess, who had been very curious about the letter ever since it arrived, came to the window. "What is it, Ossie?" she asked. He handed her the letter and she read it quickly. "Congratulations, Ossie!" she said. "But I have been publishing your drawings on my needlework for quite some time now, so I discovered you before them! I always knew you have the makings of an artist."

"Thank you, mam," said Ossie.

He was light footed as he went down the steps and out onto the road. Wait until he showed the letter to his parents! His father would probably smile reservedly and say, "But you have some money in those fingers of yours, boy!" His mother would probably make a bigger fuss and show the drawing to all her friends and church members. Then he would show the drawing (but not the cheque) to Mr. Llewellyn, who would probably show it to the class and tell them about all the great cartoonists published in the paper. Then Ossie would show it to a relieved Washie who would now have his loan repaid, and he would thank him for the confidence he had showed in him. He would thank Brightly for his encouragement regarding the post office. He wasn't sure how Phonso would react. He would probably crack some deprecating joke and then ask Ossie for his autograph. Ossie was now running on the road. The image of Uncle Basil rose up in his mind. He saw him raising his mug of beer to him, and saying: "Cheers!"

A JAMAICAN CAROL

The evening before Christmas Eve, Ossie's mother reminded him that his first task the following morning would be to go to Bushy Park to pick oranges and tangerines. The fruits would be used to 'deck the hall' for the singing which was customarily held at their home the night before Christmas. Relatives and friends would come to sing carols until daylight. They would feast on the traditional duck-shaped and round breads, on fried sprat and a variety of meats, and the beverages would include liquor for the men, as well as coffee and homemade hot chocolate which they would drink in enamel mugs.

As he lay in bed that night, Ossie thought about Bushy Park, a piece of land that his mother told him she had inherited from her father, and which was Ossie's favourite of the three properties his parents owned. In addition to the oranges and tangerines, it was also abundant with coffee, cocoa, bananas, bissy, coconuts, mangoes, pineapples and jackfruits. It was reached by following a path down into a deep valley, crossing a river, and then following the contours of several ridges before plunging into an even deeper valley. As he lay waiting for sleep to come, Ossie relived some of his memories of Bushy Park.

Once, while he was there on a chore, he heard a loud buff! He realized that a ripe jackfruit had fallen from a tree. He heard it rolling down into the bushes and he chased it. He found it resting at the riverside, and he picked it up and carried it home on his shoulder. The scent of ripe jackfruit evoked intense and opposite reactions in most people, but he was one of those who loved it. He cut the fruit open and shared the pieces with his relatives, neighbours and friends. "Before you make good food waste, make belly buss!" said Phonso, as he tackled his second slice.

Another memory was unpleasant. He was there very early one morning, and was walking downhill through the dark cocoa cultivation when a patch of bright sunshine on his right caught his attention. He looked through the trees and saw a small yellow and black bird feasting on a patch of yellow allamanda flowers. As fast as he could, he took his slingshot from around his neck, took a pebble from his pocket and loaded it in the tongue of the weapon, and then knelt on the ground and took aim. When he felt the aim was perfect he fired the pebble. It hit the bird off the flower and he saw it fall to the grass. Excited by his success, he rushed over and picked up the dead creature. He held it in his fingers. The recently sucked nectar was dripping from its tiny beak. He suddenly felt full of revulsion and remorse. One minute the bird was a beautiful thing breakfasting in the morning sunshine. A second later, due to his action, it was a dead, limp thing on the ground. And the bird was not even an edible species. He hated himself. In a fit of anger, he threw the slingshot into the bushes. He resolved there and then that he would quit this bird shooting business.

The third memory was his discovery of a deposit of clay on the bank of the river. The soil was ochre in colour, soft, clammy and very malleable. He told his father about it, and was informed that clay was used to make pots and the things they called china. He asked Mr. Llewelyn for more information, and was told that many of the bricks that were used to make buildings, especially old churches, were made from clay. People who made utensils from clay were called potters, he said, and there was a famous story about one of them in the book of

Jeremiah in the Bible. He said, further, that the ceramics industry was an important one. Artists who were called sculptors also modeled works from clay. This last bit of information was of special interest to him and he resolved that one day he would try making objects from this clay.

The following morning Ossie hurried through his breakfast of roast breadfruit, fried pork and hot chocolate, picked up his father's basket and set off for Bushy Park. After crossing the river, he began following the path which curved around a sequence of ridges. As he was passing a patch of breadfruit trees on his left, he noticed what looked like a poster high up on one of the trees. Why would anyone put a poster so high up where no one could read it from the road, he wondered? But he became very curious about what was written on the poster. So he put his basket at the side of the road and went down into the field to investigate. He climbed the tree and got to the poster. Written in pencil, and with what he thought was atrocious handwriting, unlike his own copperplate hand, he read the words on the poster:

NOTICE

TRESPASERS WILL BE PERSECUTED
By Order

The Owner.

"Oi! I catch one of dem at last!" he heard a man's voice shout from the foot of the tree.

He looked down and saw Maas Lennie glaring up at him. The whites of his eyes were flaring on his black face, and Ossie thought the red in them nearly matched that of his cap. Ossie also detected what looked like foam at the corners of his mouth.

"I can't get a single breadfruit off my property because of these so-called praedial larcenists!" he declared. "But I call them thieves, for that is what they are! And now I have one in me hands."

Ossie was now at the foot of the tree. "I was only trying to read your notice," he said. "I am on my way to Bushy Park to pick fruits for the singing."

"Then why you didn't read it from the road? Your eyes bad or what? Little boy like you and your eyes bad already? And what dem send you to school for? You mean you going to school every day and you still illegitimate?"

"'Illiterate'," said Ossie. "People who can't read are illiterate. And you have two spelling mistakes on the notice. The words should be 'TRESPASSERS' and 'PROSECUTED'".

"And him facety too!" declared Maas Lennie. "Have manners boy! You must know how to talk to big people. I am older than your father!"

"And the dictionary older than you, my father, and me," replied Ossie.

"That does it!" declared Maas Lennie. "I am making a citizen's arrest! I am taking you to Maas Rashie the D.C. You will be charged with larceny!" He grabbed Ossie by the waist of his pants.

"I don't want anybody tief my basket," said Ossie as he reached for the container.

Maas Lennie grunted his understanding as he began dragging Ossie towards the home of the constable.

They found Maas Rashie sitting on his doorstep polishing a pair of shoes. "What you doing with Maas Johnny's boy?" he demanded of Maas Lennie as soon as he dragged Ossie into the yard.

"I found him on one of my breadfruit trees. People t'iefing all my breadfruits. I can't even get one fi me Christmus."

"Why would Ossie want to steal your breadfruit when his father has enough breadfruits to stone dogs?" asked Maas Rashie.

"These young people don't follow their elders. The more they have is the more they want."

Ossie told Maas Rashie his reason for climbing the tree.

"I share your feelings about the thieves, for praedial larcenists are destroying agriculture in this country," said Maas Rashie. "But this young man is curious. He wants to find out things. That is why when you go to his home you always see him reading or drawing. So it doesn't surprise me the least that he wanted to read your stupid sign. I saw that sign myself, and I couldn't read it either! Let him go or I am going to charge you with child abuse!"

Maas Lennie quickly loosened his grip on Ossie's waist.

"Thank you Maas Rashie!" cried Ossie as he sprinted out of the yard. The sun was now high in the sky. He had to hurry to complete his chore.

A couple of chains beyond the ill-fated breadfruit tree, he saw Maas Lennie's donkey grazing on a patch of grassland on his right. He was suddenly overcome by feelings of anger against Maas Lennie. It had been very humiliating being hauled like a common criminal halfway up the hill. He decided to take revenge. He loosened the rope of Maas Lennie's donkey. Then he continued running towards Bushy Park.

The memory of the 'arrest' and his mixed feelings about loosening the donkey spoiled his anticipated pleasure of climbing the trees and picking the fragrant fruits. But he picked enough oranges and tangerines to fill the basket. Then he remembered the clay. He went down to the stream and used his penknife to dig up some of the clammy substance; then he wrapped it in a tania leaf and added it to the basket. He wasn't sure what kind of Christmas object he would make with the clay, but he felt sure he would think of something.

As he approached the patch of grass where he had loosened the donkey, he saw the free animal walking towards him. He felt rising remorse about what he had done. What if the animal destroyed other people's crops? He would be responsible. So he grabbed the donkey's rope and decided that he would re-tether him on the same lump of grass. But as he approached the spot, he saw Maas Lennie standing there and looking around for the lost animal as he shouted her name:

"Genny! Genny! Genny!"

"See her here, sah!" said Ossie.

"Oh is you! Thanks for finding her. I am so relieved! I was only trying to frighten you, boy. I wouldn't let them put you in prison or reform school."

Ossie said nothing and continued walking.

His unease was slightly lessened by the delicious lunch that his mother served: green gungo peas and saltfish and tomatoes cooked down in coconut milk to a custard, and accompanied with slices of yellow yam and boiled green bananas. He washed it down with a glass of homemade sorrel. But some of the cloud of the morning's events still hung over him.

He turned to decorating the hall with the fruits. As he hung them on the nails that were kept from year to year, he enjoyed their colours and scents, for they also reminded him of previous Christmases. He knew from the cards that his parents received that many people decorated their homes with Christmas trees. But the only real one he had ever seen was at Mr. Llewellyn's home, and the teacher had told him that the Christmas tree was a very ancient custom which probably had something to do with the desire of European people to have some greenery in their homes during the ice and cold of the long winters. Historians disagreed about it, he said, but somehow Christians gradually adopted it as a symbol of the birth of Christ. The tree came to the island when the English conquerors brought their customs with them. But most people just enjoyed the colours and lights, beauty and atmosphere of it, without giving much thought to its history. This was his reason for having one, he said. Ossie told him a story he had heard from Uncle Basil. During his first winter in Europe he was sitting inside and he looked through the window at a pine tree with snow on its branches, and it occurred to him that such an image was natural for the people there, for it was what they saw around them at this time of year. Even the clothes the people wore resembled those he had seen on Christmas cards. The real snow on the tree was so different from the cotton Jamaicans put on theirs to imitate snow. Mr. Llewellyn admitted that he himself had never seen snow for he had never left the island, but it was something he hoped to see some day. Ossie said that the snowballs he bought at church functions were the nearest he had come to seeing snow. He continued hanging the fruits and reflected that the advantage of his family tradition was that people could eat the fruits. Who ever heard of anyone eating a Christmas tree?

Feeling a little better now, he went out to the verandah to work on his lump of clay. He took a piece of board from the kitchen, an old table top, and rested it on his lap. He covered the board with sheets of an old newspaper and rested the clay on them. Then he began to think. What would be the best image for Christmas? He thought of Santa Claus, but his belief in him had come to a sudden end when he realized that they did not have a chimney on their house, and that he had caught his mother buying the things at the shop that had turned up in his stocking. Then he thought of the jingle bells, but the only bells he knew were church-bells and bicycle bells, and they had nothing specifically to do with Christmas. Then he remembered the Jonkunnu band that had scared the daylights out of him while he was spending Christmas with Aunt Ruby in Kingston. He remembered them vividly—Mr. Llewellyn once told him that he had a photographic memory—and he could remember Pitchy-Patchy, the Belly-Woman, the Policeman and others. But something else also came to his mind. Once while discussing Jamaican Christmas traditions, Mr. Llewellyn had showed the class a reproduction of a painting of Jonkunnu masqueraders done by a 19th century artist named Belisario. He remembered the name for it was a very unusual one, not like Johnson, Smith and McDonald, the common names in his district. Mr. Llewellyn had seemed proud of the widely held belief that this man was the very first native born Jamaican artist of reknown. He remembered the central image in the painting, a character called Koo-Koo or Actor Boy, a black man wearing a white mask, the longhair of Europeans, and very fancy clothes, and who, during the masquerade, recited verses from Shakespeare and other great British poets. It seemed to Ossie that the Christmas trees, carols, bells, balloons, firecrackers and the like, were very much in the tradition of the Actor Boy' recitations. He decided that the Actor Boy would be the subject for his piece, and he went to work.

The bust which he produced was not merely an imitation of Belisario's painting. He took the idea of a black man wearing a white mask, and sculpted a man with a very Negroid head who was wearing a white mask and a wig of European hair. He used paint from his set to colour the mask. He retained the three-pronged headpiece, for he thought that it may have been a Jonkunnu tradition, as well as the costume at the shoulders, for these, he felt, may have been the fashion at the time.

"Is what dat, Ossie?" his mother asked when he showed it to her. He explained what he was trying to do.

"Put it on the centre table," she said, "and put the Christmas cards behind it as background."

Ossie got busy as he followed his mother's instructions, and as he tried to show his work with the best possible anticipated effect.

By the time he finished dinner–green gungo peas soup with smoked pork, carrots and yellow yam, and followed by a gizada–he was ready for the singing to begin. He bathed and got dressed. His mother was busy preparing the food. His father was setting up a little bar in the corner of the living room.

At around 8:00p.m. Maas Peng was the first to arrive. He sat on one of the chairs on the verandah. He was a man of many tragedies, including being hit on the head by a falling ripe breadfruit and being covered by a landslide, but his field bore the biggest yams in the district, including one on which the villagers said they saw the face of Jesus.

"What would you like to drink, Maas Peng?" asked Maas Johnnie.

"Gimme a sorrel, nuh," he replied.

"I am surprised, for I know you can be quite a water bird," said Maas Johnny.

"I am slowing down for the Christmus," said Maas Peng.

Maas Johnny went to get the drink.

Aunt Ruby, Miss Ona's sister, and a postal clerk in Kingston, was the next to arrive. She had driven up to Clifton in her "brand new second hand car", as she described it, and she would spend Christmas with them and return to the city on Boxing Day. She was an extroverted woman, and her love of fun and laughter lit up the frequent smile on her light-brown, freckled face. As usual, she embarrassed Ossie by loudly insisting on kissing him. A demanding woman, she also insisted that he say the grace at every meal. But he loved the gifts she always brought. This time she gave him a mouth organ, some balloons, and a Christmas hat with the words "Christmus a Come" printed and pasted on the front. She went into the kitchen to greet and chat with Miss Ona. A few minutes later she returned to the verandah carrying a glass of sorrel she had collected from Maas Johnny. She sat and chatted with Maas Peng for a few minutes, then returned to the kitchen to help Miss Ona with the food.

Uncle Phil was the next to arrive. A failed barber who was now doing well as a shoemaker, he apologized to Maas Johnny for the absence of his wife Gloria who had to stay home to take care of a sick child. He opted for a white rum with coconut water, for he said he needed it to keep him warm in the Christmas breeze that was blowing across the hills and valleys. Furthermore, he quipped, he was a Churchillian on matters alcoholic: in defeat he needed it, and in victory he deserved it, and he had been victorious that year with his shoemaking. He sat beside Maas Peng and received his rum with loudly expressed gratitude.

Miss Princess began shouting, "Merry Christmas everyone!" while she was still walking down the path. Then she stood, smiling, in front of the verandah. People called her a near-white woman, but Ossie wondered why no one ever described someone as near-black.

"Welcome Miss Princess!" said Maas Johnny. "Please have a seat."

"Thank you, but I want to have a word with Miss Ona first. She probably needs help in the kitchen."

She went off to join her friend, but stopped in the living room to look at Ossie's sculpture. "Ossie, come here. You made this?"

"Yes mam," said Ossie as he joined her inside.

"Tell me about it," she requested. He explained as best as he could, feeling as always, that the piece spoke best for itself.

"I think it is probably your best piece," she said. "I am used to your drawings, but never saw you sculpt anything before."

"It is my first," said Ossie.

"Do a drawing of it for me," she said. "I like it very much."

"Yes mam," replied Ossie, very pleased with her usual enthusiasm for his work. She went to spend time with Miss Ona in the kitchen, and she later rejoined the others on the verandah, with a bottle of Pepsi from the bar in her hand, always her favourite drink, Christmas or no Christmas, she said.

Paulette, wearing a blue dress, brought a cake from Mama D. She took it into the kitchen to Miss Ona. Ossie overheard her apologies for Mama D's absence, and the instructions that the lump of icing sugar was specially for him.

"Tell Mama D thanks for me," he said to Paulette when she joined him in the living room.

"You must also make sure to thank her yourself," said Paulette as she sat down beside him. "What is this?" she asked looking at his sculpture.

"My latest work, "said Ossie.

Paulette studied it carefully. "It looks deep," she said.

"Popsi the magician is here!" they heard Uncle Phil say on the verandah.

"Greetings to the I dem!" Popsi replied.

"So you going to do any magic for us tonight?" asked Uncle Phil.

"No, man. Christmas is the greatest magic. Nobody can top that."

They saw Maas Johnny come into the living room for the rum and ginger that Popsi had ordered, then he returned to the verandah with the drink.

They heard Phonso, Washie and Brightly greeting the adults very politely on the verandah. "Where is Ossie?" asked Washie.

"In the living room," replied Aunt Ruby. They came in, and now that they were out of their khaki school uniforms, they seemed free and happy. Washie wore a light-blue turtleneck shirt and blue jeans. Brightly wore a red and white check shirt and grey pants. Phonso boasted a bright yellow shirt and blue pants. They sat down.

"Look at Ossie's sculpture," said Paulette.

"Is what?" asked Washie.

"A Jonkunnu head," said Paulette.

"Oh? Those ugly frightening people?" Washie responded. "But this one not so ugly. But the mask frighten me a little bit."

"You must get the meaning," said Paulette.

"I see a black man wearing a mask," said Brightly.

"I never see Jonkunnu yet," said Phonso. "But I hear about them. Ossie always doing art. He seems to have something for every occasion. Even in the holidays."

"Hark the Herald Angels Sing!" It was Maas Rashie singing as he approached the verandah. "I wish you all a lawful Christmas," he said, evoking chuckles on the verandah. Then he entered the living room. "Merry Christmas little ones."

"Merry Christmas Maas Rashie," they chorused.

"Larry is behind bars waiting to be tried for murder," he said. "I wonder what he is thinking now?"

"People pay Christmas visits to prisons," said Paulette. "I read about it in the newspaper."

Ossie reflected on his tragic friend who sought redemption in the hard work of digging potato hills. A terrible fate could await him. This made Ossie very sad.

"For unto us a child is born!" sang Maas Lennie as he approached the verandah.

"Mr. Christie, I have a good mind throwing you out of my house!" declared Maas Johnny. "I heard what you did to my boy."

"Oh, I wasn't going to hurt him. You have to be tough and strong with the younger generation. They must learn to respect private property. And a boy shouldn't be too soft. He must learn to take rough-up."

Miss Ona left the kitchen and sped through the living room to the verandah to confront Maas Lennie. "Is it because you have no children of your own, Leonard?" she demanded from him.

"My father never spared the supple-jack with me," said Maas Lennie. "If I missed a step, he beat me within an inch of my life."

"He may have got that from slavery," said Maas Johnny. "But we are not slaves anymore."

Ossie wondered how his parents knew about the incident, for he hadn't told them, and neither had mentioned it to him. But there was a saying in the district that 'bush have ears'. So the 'bush-telegram', as the old people called it, had been at work.

"Nevertheless pour him a drink," said Miss Ona. "Is Christmus."

"So what would you like to drink, Lennie?" asked Maas Johnny.

"I will have a whiskey and soda," replied Maas Lennie and there was laughter on the verandah. "Make it a white rum on the rocks," he added. He entered the living room and sat beside Maas Rashie. Maas Johnnie served him the drink.

"It was me who let-go your donkey," Ossie confessed to Maas Lennie.

"Really? You wanted revenge. I understand that very well."

"I will make a new sign for you," said Ossie.

"Really? Thank you very much. I wasn't good at drawing at school. And I only made it to second class."

"O Come All Ye Faithful!" sang Maas Peng on the verandah. The others joined in. Maas Johnny went into the bedroom and returned with his guitar. He sat beside Maas Rashie and quickly fell in tune. Miss Ona came from the kitchen and sat beside the children. The singing was on its way.

After a few rounds of carols, Miss Ona went to the bedroom and returned with her Bible and her glasses. She put on the glasses, leaned close to the lamp, and turned the pages of the Bible.

"Attention everyone!" she called out. In the silence that followed she read Luke's account of The Annunciation, her voice sometimes faltering because of the weak light. "Amen!" everyone chorused when she was finished.

They resumed caroling. About an hour before midnight the women served the food and the hot beverages. As they ate they discussed many topics from farming matters to national politics. Over and over the conversation returned to memories of old time Christmases.

But Ossie felt himself getting very sleepy. It had been a very full day. And the Christmas Day itself that he had looked forward to for an entire year, would soon be upon him. He needed rest for it. So he went inside, put on his pajamas and went to bed.

Although he was very tired, sleep did not come. He could overhear the conversation going on in the living room. Miss Princess had invited those on the verandah to join those inside and look at his sculpture.

"I have been noticing that graven image," said Maas Lennie with traces of the commandment against them sounding in his voice.

"The boy could one day be a successful artist," replied Miss Princess.

"The head is quite life-like," said Maas Peng.

"Masked men always scare me a bit," said Aunt Ruby. "But it is so well done."

"I don't know what he is going to do with it, but the boy has a gift," said his mother.

"The Gleaner paid him for a drawing," said his father.

"Really?" said Uncle Phil. "I wonder if it pays more than shoe-making?"

There was laughter.

Ossie dozed. He was awakened by their enthusiastic singing of "We Wish You a Merry Christmas!" Then he heard Miss Princess and Phonso praising the sweetness of the oranges and tangerines. He recalled that his mother would soon be waking him up to go to the early morning Christmas service. He was listening to the Christmas breeze blowing as sleep stole him away.

When the Christmas celebrations were over Ossie made the promised sign for Maas Lennie. He got some board and house paint from his father. He attached a stake to it so the sign could be planted on the bank overlooking the breadfruit trees. The sign read:

NOTICE

TRESPASSERS WILL BE PROSECUTED
BY ORDER

Leonard B. Christie Esq.
PROPRIETOR.

ABOUT THE AUTHOR

St. Hope Earl McKenzie is a Jamaican creative writer, visual artist and academic philosopher. A graduate of Mico College and Columbia University, he also holds a PhD in Philosophy from the University of British Columbia. He is a former head of the Department of English at Church Teachers' College, and taught Philosophy at the University of the West Indies, Mona. The author of fourteen books, including collections of short stories, volumes of poetry, a memoir, a novel, a multi-genre collection and books of philosophy, he was awarded a Silver Musgrave Medal by the Institute of Jamaica for outstanding merit in the field of literature.

www.ingramcontent.com/pod-product-compliance
Lightning Source LLC
Chambersburg PA
CBHW050833180626
46814CB00004B/1592